*"You test me," J.D. g[...]
tempt me. What are you thinking,
letting me do this?"*

Kirby's eyes went wide. "You wanted—I
thought—"

He took a step back from her. She was gratified to
see that his hand trembled ever so slightly. The
sight of that tiny weakness gave her courage.

"I wanted to kiss you," she whispered. "And you
wanted to kiss me."

"And do you always give men what they want?" he
asked.

She gasped.

"I'm sorry." He bent his head. "I should never have
said that." With a bitter oath, he whirled away.

"Where are you going?" she cried, contrite.

"I've got to get out of here before I do something
we'll both regret."

Perhaps his words should have frightened her, but
as the door slammed behind him, she felt only a
burning regret that he'd left.

Dear Reader,

April is the time for the little things...a time for nature to nurture new growth, a time for spring to begin to show its glory.

So, it's perfect timing to have a THAT'S MY BABY! title this month. *What To Do About Baby* by award-winning author Martha Hix is a tender, humorous tale about a heroine who discovers love in the most surprising ways. After her estranged mother's death, the last thing Caroline Grant expected to inherit was an eighteen-month-old sister...or to fall in love with the handsome stranger who delivered the surprise bundle!

And more springtime fun is in store for our readers as Sherryl Woods's wonderful series THE BRIDAL PATH continues with the delightful *Danielle's Daddy Factor*. Next up, Pamela Toth's BUCKLES & BRONCOS series brings you back to the world of the beloved Buchanan brothers when their long-lost sister, Kirby, is found—and is about to discover romance in *Buchanan's Return*.

What is spring without a wedding? *Stop the Wedding!* by Trisha Alexander is sure to win your heart! And don't miss Janis Reams Hudson's captivating story of reunited lovers in *The Mother of His Son*. And a surefire keeper is coming your way in *A Stranger to Love* by Patricia McLinn. This tender story promises to melt your heart!

I hope you enjoy each and every story this month!

Sincerely,

Tara Gavin,
Senior Editor

Please address questions and book requests to:
Silhouette Reader Service
U.S.: 3010 Walden Ave., P.O. Box 1325, Buffalo, NY 14269
Canadian: P.O. Box 609, Fort Erie, Ont. L2A 5X3

PAMELA TOTH
BUCHANAN'S RETURN

Published by Silhouette Books

America's Publisher of Contemporary Romance

To F.J.B., with love, for showing me that romantic
heroes really do exist.

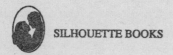 SILHOUETTE BOOKS

ISBN 0-373-24096-1

BUCHANAN'S RETURN

Copyright © 1997 by Pamela Toth

This edition published by arrangement with Harlequin Books S.A.

® and TM are trademarks of Harlequin Books S.A., used under license.
Trademarks indicated with ® are registered in the United States Patent
and Trademark Office, the Canadian Trade Marks Office and in other
countries.

Printed in U.S.A.

PAMELA TOTH

was born in Wisconsin but grew up in Seattle, where she attended the University of Washington and majored in art. She still lives near Seattle and she has two daughters, several Siamese cats and a dwarf hamster named Brutus. When she isn't writing, she enjoys reading, traveling, quilting and researching new story ideas.

The heroes of her books have won several *Romantic Times* W.I.S.H. awards, and she has been nominated for five *Romantic Times* Reviewer's Choice awards, including Best Series Romance for *Walk Away, Joe.* Her books appear regularly at the top of the Waldenbooks Romance Bestseller list, and *Buchanan's Baby* was on the *USA Today* list.

She loves hearing from readers, and can be reached at P.O. Box 5845, Bellevue, WA 98006. For a personal reply, a stamped, self-addressed envelope is appreciated.

WYOMING

NEBRASKA

KANSAS

UTAH

COLORADO

Fort Collins

Sterling

Caulder Springs

Nederland • Boulder
Vail
★ Denver
Aspen
The Rocking Rose Ranch

Colorado Springs

N

ARIZONA   NEW MEXICO   OKLAHOMA

All underlined places are fictitious.

Prologue

Boise, Idaho

"You can open your eyes now. I'm all finished." Setting the glass vial aside, Kirby Wilson swabbed the small wound on the inside of Pete Graham's elbow and covered it with a bandage.

Pete blinked and released the breath he'd been holding. "I'm glad that's over." Grinning sheepishly, he stood and rolled down the sleeve of his work shirt.

"Call back on Friday for the results," Kirby told him. At least Pete had been too distracted by the sight of his own blood to ask her out. Ever since news of Kirby's divorce had gotten around, Pete, who worked as foreman for the Boise street department, had been coming to the medical clinic a couple of times a month with minor injuries. When he did, he always asked Kirby for a date. Since the sight of blood, especially his own, made his normally florid face turn alarmingly pale, she had to admire his persistence.

Still, it wasn't enough to keep her from turning down his invitations. Sooner or later he would realize she wasn't interested and give up.

"Uh, Kirby…" Pete began as she was about to leave the examination room.

Her hand tightened on the doorknob and she pasted a regretful smile on her face. There was nothing wrong with the man; she just wasn't ready to start dating again.

"Kirby," the receptionist, Jill Palmer, called from the hallway before Pete could continue. "If you're all done, would you come here for a minute? There's someone waiting to see you."

Relieved at the interruption, Kirby excused herself hastily and slipped out the door. *Coward!* she thought as she did.

"Who is it?" she asked Jill.

As well as being the receptionist for the clinic where Kirby had worked for the last four years, Jill had also become her best friend. Now she was wearing a strange expression. She didn't even echo Pete Graham's goodbye as he passed her on his way out.

"The man's name is Donovan Buchanan," she replied as soon as the front door shut behind Pete. "I thought you might want some privacy, so I put him in the doctor's office."

Kirby knew that Dr. Gilpin was at a meeting downtown. The waiting room was deserted. She had no idea who her visitor was and she wondered why Jill assumed she'd want privacy.

Before Kirby could ask, the phone rang. As Jill

reached for the receiver, Kirby automatically patted the long blond hair she wore fastened in a clip at her nape and went back down the hall.

When she entered the doctor's inner office, she saw a tall, golden-haired man in jeans and a suede jacket standing at the window with his back to her. A brown Stetson dangled from one hand and he wore cowboy boots.

Kirby had just enough time to admire his long legs and the width of his shoulders before he turned to face her.

When he did, her greeting died in her throat. His eyes, the same green as her own, narrowed as he returned her stare.

"My God," he muttered, looking slightly dazed. "It *is* you."

Kirby took a step backward, biting her lip. There was something about this stranger that caused alarm to flutter in her chest.

"What do you mean? And why did you want to see me?"

Still staring, he swallowed hard. Then a huge grin broke out beneath his full mustache and he gave his head a shake. "I can hardly believe I've found you," he said, confusing her further. "Honey, don't you recognize me? I'm your brother, Donnie Buchanan."

Chapter One

"Are you a real cowboy?"

J. D. Reese shifted in his seat at the Denver airline terminal, returning the curious stare of a small boy who appeared to be about four years old. Taking off his battered Stetson, J.D. smoothed a hand over the long black hair he wore pulled back and tied with a leather thong.

"I reckon I used to be a cowboy," he drawled, thinking of his days as a rodeo rough-stock rider. "Now I guess I'm just an Indian." Actually, J.D. was only a quarter Navajo, on his mother's side. "Part Indian, anyway," he amended.

The little boy took a step backward and looked him over with interest. "Which part?"

"Michael! Come over here right now."

As the child scampered away, J.D. clamped the hat back on his head and exchanged glances with the attractive brunette he figured must be the boy's mother. When he saw her face tighten with disapproval, he resisted the urge to tell her that he hadn't scalped anyone in weeks. Instead, he pinned her with an expressionless stare.

The woman's eyes widened at his insolence and then color ran up her cheeks as she grabbed the little boy's hand. Scolding as they went, she dragged him away down the airport concourse.

J.D. crossed his booted feet and worried the toothpick tucked into the corner of his mouth as he waited for his boss to arrive on the flight from Boise. People hurried by, paying him no more mind than if he'd been carved from a block of wood. Idly, he watched an assortment of luggage and other items begin spilling onto the rotating baggage carousel. Two pairs of skis went past, followed by a battered cardboard box tied with twine and several expensive-looking suitcases.

A crowd was coming in his direction. The boss was bringing his sister to stay at the ranch for a while and J.D. wondered if she was pretty.

Not that he cared. He spent most of his time around horses and ranch hands no more talkative than he was, and he liked it that way. Any woman, pretty or plain, would only be an unwelcome distraction.

At least he wouldn't be the one stuck entertaining her.

As he waited, J.D. itched for a cigarette. Quitting was hell and the mint-flavored toothpick was a poor substitute for the sharp bite of tobacco. Sometimes quitting hardly seemed worth the effort.

"J.D.!" called a deep, familiar voice. "Over here." Head sticking above the other passengers straggling toward the baggage area, Donovan Buchanan waved his hand. Beside him J.D. glimpsed a woman with long blond hair.

J.D. got to his feet and maneuvered his way through the stream of people, his bad hip throbbing dully with each step he took. The ranch's newest four-legged boarder had caught him by surprise this morning, shying at a sudden noise and slamming him against the wall of the stall with her spotted rump.

"You okay?" Buchanan asked when J.D. reached him.

A sharp nod was J.D.'s only reply. He disliked being reminded of his injury. It was bad enough that he'd been forced to accept Buchanan's charity; the rancher's pity was more than J.D. could stomach. In the six months he had been in Colorado, he'd made no attempt to hide the fact that the other man's gratitude stuck in his craw like a chicken bone.

"I'd like you to meet my sister." Buchanan grinned, undaunted by J.D.'s black expression. "Kirby, this is J.D. Reese, the best horse trainer in Colorado. J.D., Kirby Wilson."

Ignoring the other man's flattery, J.D. looked at the woman standing beside him. Her long, wavy hair was the color of fireweed honey, a couple shades darker than her brother's, and her green eyes were almond shaped, like a cat's, above a full, smiling mouth.

Involuntary reaction to her appearance sizzled through him, worsening his already bad mood. The last thing he needed was a case of the hots for his boss's new kin.

Right now her cat's eyes were crinkled with humor, making J.D. wonder if she could sense his response.

A woman with her looks would be used to stirring up some kind of reaction in a man.

"Nice to meet you, Mr. Reese." Her voice was pleasantly husky, her tone friendly. The top of her head reached only Buchanan's shoulder, and she wore a belted red parka with blue jeans.

J.D. yanked his attention away from her sweetly curving mouth and clamped down hard on his unwilling awareness of her charms. Automatically touching his fingers to the brim of his hat, he returned her greeting with a silent nod.

The horse trainer's unsmiling expression and dark eyes, as cold as black ice, made Kirby drop the hand she'd been about to extend. Pride kept her chin high and her smile bland until he looked back at Donovan.

"How was the trip?" Reese asked.

"A total success."

When the trainer had been walking toward them through the crowd of deplaning passengers, Kirby noticed that he moved with a limp. Being a nurse, she wondered about its cause. Being a woman, she appreciated his rugged, untamed appearance, even if his manners did seem to be equally unpolished.

He was nearly as tall as her golden-haired brother and obviously in good shape, despite the limp. Like many of the men she'd seen in the crowded airport, he wore Western clothes and a cowboy hat. Beneath it, straight dark hair was tied at his nape. He had cheekbones a model would kill for and a nose that must have been broken at least once, giving his face the kind of appeal that perfection never did. His skin was weathered to a rich bronze, his jeans faded below an equally worn denim jacket that hung open over a flannel shirt.

When J.D. caught her staring, his black brows rose mockingly. Refusing to be intimidated, Kirby raised her own.

"Doesn't she remind you of Rose?" Donovan asked. He had shown Kirby the snapshot of his daughter that he carried in his wallet. Rose was five and looked like him.

Something glittered in J.D.'s dark eyes as he took a step back and studied Kirby from head to foot. Heat bloomed on her cheeks at his leisurely appraisal, and she barely resisted the urge to fold her arms protectively across her chest.

"Naw, she looks older," J.D. drawled when he was done staring. He knew he was treading on dangerous ground. Being good enough to train the man's horses didn't mean it was okay for a 'breed like J.D. to lust after his sister. The perversity in J.D.'s nature couldn't resist a poke to see if he'd stir up any hornets.

"Oh, come on, man," Buchanan protested affably. "Use your imagination. I only meant that Rose looks just like Kirby did as a child."

"If that's the case, you'd better have a shotgun handy when Rose grows up," J.D. replied without thinking. "You're going to need it."

Kirby's eyes widened as she took in his meaning, and then she dropped her gaze as if she had no idea how pretty she was. "Thanks, I think," she mumbled.

"You may have a point." Buchanan's tone didn't carry any underlying warning that J.D. could detect. He hadn't figured out his boss's attitude yet, and that made him wary. He glared at Kirby when she raised her eyes, and then he directed his irritation at the rancher.

"I've got stalls to clean." J.D. shifted impatiently, jerking his head toward the luggage carousel. "How many bags did you bring?"

Buchanan glanced at his sister. "You want to wait here while we grab 'em?"

"Sure." Her smile seemed to include J.D. He nearly returned it before he remembered himself. A short while later, as the three of them walked through the late-fall chill to the car, he made a pretence of ignoring her, but the sound of her voice as she replied to Buchanan's comments was as impossible to shut out as was the image of her sparkling cat's eyes and her sweetly tempting lips.

"Anything happen at home that I need to know about?" Donovan asked J.D. when they had left the airport behind and were driving east.

The trainer's head didn't turn as he steered the sedan down the flat, straight road. "I doubt it."

If Donovan had expected a more detailed reply from his hired hand, Kirby couldn't tell as she listened idly from the back seat while studying the view through the car window. From the western horizon behind them, the majestic Rockies rose in a faint, jagged line. In every other direction, the prairie stretched flat, brown and empty except for an occasional clump of trees. Overhead, a single plane bisected the pale sky. Kirby found the stark landscape calming in its simplicity, as if its vastness would give a person all the room she needed without ever making her feel closed in. It was certainly a change from Boise.

In the warmth of the car, fatigue weighted her eyelids, but she struggled against it. The events of the last few days had worn her out emotionally, and she longed for a nap, but she didn't want to miss a single detail of her visit.

"How's the stock?" Donovan asked J.D. Back in Boise, he had explained to Kirby that he bred a small number of Appaloosa horses as well as running cattle.

"Fine. The cut on Ringo's foreleg is healing. The buyer from Denver came and picked Pagan up yesterday. The blacksmith stopped by—so did the vet." J.D.'s voice droned on as if he were reciting a school lesson. "Candy's eye is cleared up. Lottie's quit trying to kick in her stall door."

"How'd you manage that?" Donovan asked when he stopped for breath.

"Moved one of the half-grown barn cats in with her. The two of them are damned near inseparable. Sorry, ma'am," he added, without taking a breath.

Ma'am? Kirby thought.

Donovan glanced around at her. "I told you he was good. Lotta Dotta's been fussing since we weaned her last foal, and nothing else has worked."

"She must have been lonesome," Kirby replied. "Was it her first foal?" She didn't know much about horses, but having a baby taken away from you every year had to be traumatic, even for an animal.

For a moment, J.D.'s gaze met hers in the rearview mirror. "No, it was her third," he said. "Perhaps she was just bored, but the cat seems to have calmed her."

Kirby wasn't sure what to say, so she remained silent.

"I'm glad it's helped." Donovan smoothed one thumb over his mustache. "I've got her bred to Pathfinder, my stud, and I wouldn't want anything to go wrong," he explained to Kirby.

"I remember reading about a gorilla that had a pet kitten," she blurted, and then she felt slightly foolish. They raised horses, not apes.

"I remember that story," J.D. replied, surprising her. "The gorilla had been taught sign language and she named the kitten herself."

"That's right." Some of Kirby's incredulity must have been evident in her voice, because he didn't volunteer anything more, even when her brother asked several questions. Had she somehow offended J.D., or had he just lost interest? She wasn't sure, and his gaze didn't stray to the mirror again.

After a moment, Donovan turned the conversation back to the ranch. Kirby noticed that he talked to J.D. as an equal rather than employer-employee, even deferring to the trainer's opinion more than once. But the talk of training schedules, worming and corrective shoes failed to hold her attention for long.

"How's Fanfare settling in?" her brother asked as they sped down the highway.

"I've got her under control." After J.D.'s brief reply, the silence dragged until it became obvious that no more details were forthcoming.

"I figured you did," Donovan said dryly. He turned to Kirby. "Fanfare's a leopard-spotted Appaloosa in foal to a grand champion from Texas," he explained. "I bought her from a breeder down there."

"I'll look forward to seeing her." Kirby hadn't been around horses since she was a child, and she couldn't picture a horse that was spotted like a leopard.

"Do you ride?" Donovan asked her.

"It's been years." She was reluctant to admit that she had been on a horse only a few times, but perhaps it would come back to her—like riding a bicycle. Not that she was going to be staying at the ranch long enough for her riding ability or lack thereof to matter, she realized.

"J.D. can fix you up with a gentle mount, can't you, J.D.?"

Buchanan's question caught him off guard and he had to struggle not to seek out Kirby's reflection in the rearview mirror. She'd made her opinion of him plain with her obvious shock that he'd read about that damned gorilla. Did she assume that a former rodeo bum must be illiterate?

"Yeah, sure, I'll find her a horse to ride." For a moment, J.D. amused himself with the idea of fixing her up with one of the retired broncs the boss had rescued from the slaughterhouse. Then he sobered. When he'd ridden bulls, the buckle bunnies who hung around the arena had treated him like a superstar, and now it came as a shock to a woman that he was even able to read.

Damn, but he'd like to show her what else he could do, he thought with a humorless twist of his lips. No doubt if he so much as laid a finger on her, though, she'd go running to her brother.

Paying Buchanan back for the charity he'd rammed down J.D.'s throat was a tempting idea, but one he couldn't afford to indulge. Too bad—the sister was a looker, and the idea of scoring off both her and her brother at the same time appealed to J.D.'s no-doubt terminally twisted sense of irony.

The next time he permitted himself a quick glance in the mirror, Kirby winked. Startled, he stared until he realized his mouth was hanging open. Did she find some secret amusement in baiting him?

When he looked at Buchanan's baby sister, humor was the last thing on J.D.'s mind.

Apparently his boss had missed the silent exchange. "Kirby's only planning to stay at the ranch for a couple of weeks," he said, voice rough, "but I'm hell-bent on changing her mind. We've got years to catch up on."

J.D.'s old man had cut out before he was born. He and his mother had lived with her father on the Navajo reservation until Grandpa Chee Whitehorse passed on to the spirit world, and now she was gone as well. He couldn't imagine what it would be like to have a sister; he only knew he was damn glad he and Kirby weren't related, for the feelings she stirred in him without even trying would have been downright incestuous.

"I do have a job waiting for me back in Boise," she was telling her brother. "I was lucky the doctor's wife was willing to fill in for me as it is."

"Kirby's a nurse," Buchanan told J.D., as if he were a part of their conversation or gave two hoots what she did.

He tried to think of something to say, but his mind got hung up on the image of her in a snug white uniform with a short skirt, revealing legs that went on forever.

A pickup passed them, going too fast. J.D. reminded himself that none of this was any of his business and tried to focus on the road. Kirby must have leaned forward. As he steered the car around a sweeping curve, he caught her scent—something light and flowery that reminded him of sunshine and summer heat. Briefly, his nostrils flared.

Out of the corner of his eye, he saw Buchanan's

hand cover hers where it rested on his shoulder. A muscle jumped in his boss's cheek and his mustache twitched as he smiled. For a moment, neither spoke, and J.D. felt like a third wheel.

"How'd you find her?" he asked, surprising himself. He'd heard of the missing sister, but he didn't know why they'd lost touch.

"Pokey Tate, a steer wrestler from Wichita, got his arm broke in Boise when the doggy balked. He went to the clinic where Kirby was working to get patched up," Buchanan said. "When I ran into him, he mentioned that he'd seen a nurse who could've been my twin."

He stopped and cleared his throat while J.D. glanced at the two of them. The resemblance was easy to see; Kirby was as pretty as Buchanan was handsome.

J.D. wondered if she had known about her missing brothers and whether she'd looked for them over the years. He'd never liked answering personal questions, though, so he'd gotten out of the habit of asking them.

When the horse trainer didn't say anything more, Kirby found she was disappointed at his lack of curiosity. Right now she was too tired to figure out why his disinterest bothered her, though; she needed a nap before she met anyone else.

Closing her eyes, she took a deep, slow breath. Her emotions were still too raw, she realized, but a good night's sleep would go a long way toward restoring them.

She woke when she felt the car slow for a turn. Blinking, she looked around curiously, but the scenery hadn't changed much. It was still brown; it just wasn't quite as flat as before and there were more trees.

"We'll be on ranch property in a few minutes," Donovan told her.

Smiling at the enthusiasm in his voice, she closed her eyes again. Part of her was eager to meet Bobbie and Rose; part of her was still gasping at the speed with which her world had turned completely upside down. For a woman who usually took her time deciding between two colors of toilet paper, she'd certainly leaped without looking into this situation.

The car slowed, turning between two redbrick pillars and driving over a cattle guard before it headed down a long dirt road.

"Welcome to the Rocking Rose," Donovan said with quiet pride.

"Named for your daughter," Kirby guessed. "What a sweet idea."

"My daughter and your niece," Donovan commented. "She's sure excited about meeting a brand-new aunt."

A sudden lump formed in Kirby's throat. "I'm looking forward to meeting her, as well." It was still difficult to believe there were so many relatives whose existence she hadn't even suspected a short week ago. What would they think of her? she wondered with a growing case of stage fright. Would they be disappointed? Would they like her?

As she clasped her hands tightly to stop their sudden trembling, the car approached a large house, freshly painted white, with blue shutters and redbrick trim.

"It's beautiful," she murmured sincerely as they drove on past it and pulled up by the back door. She barely had time to notice several other buildings farther down the lane before the door to the house burst open. A little girl wearing a pink parka hurried down the steps, followed by a slim, pretty brunette Kirby recognized from her brother's wedding picture.

"Bobbie's going to adore you," he said, sliding out of the car before it came to a complete stop. He held out his arms, hugging Rose with one as he caught his wife close with the other and kissed her firmly on her upturned mouth.

Watching them through the car window, Kirby experienced a rush of envy. Since the end of her three-year marriage, she'd been alone. Seeing the way Donovan's family greeted him, she felt more lonely than ever—despite the new relatives she was about to meet.

Shyness gripped her and she remained where she was until the car door was opened and J.D. leaned down to study her with a solemn expression on his darkly handsome face.

"You okay?"

The question surprised her. She swallowed the lump of nerves in her throat and nodded as she slid across the seat toward the door. "Sure." Her voice sounded a little weak. Where was her normal self-assurance when she needed it? "I'm fine."

To her surprise, J.D. extended a hand to assist her, his grip warm and firm through her glove. His unreadable gaze remained intent on hers.

"They don't bite," he said quietly as he let her go.

Kirby's eyes widened. Had she heard him correctly? How had this man picked up on her sudden nervousness when her own brother was oblivious to her discomfort? Did J.D., too, sometimes feel like an intruder?

There wasn't time to ask, or to thank him for his quiet encouragement, before he walked around to the rear of the car and opened the trunk.

"Hi, J.D.!" Rose's voice shattered the spell around Kirby as the horse trainer leaned down to give the little girl a hug. Fascinated by the family resemblance, Kirby stared at her niece.

"Hi, yourself, Tulip," J.D. replied.

"My name's not Tulip," she protested with a giggle. "I'm Rose. You know that."

Kirby was amazed at the grin that transformed J.D.'s harsh features. His fathomless eyes were crinkled with laughter, the hard line of his mouth for once relaxed and surprisingly sensual.

And she'd thought he was attractive before!

"I keep forgetting," he teased Rose with mock regret. "I'll just have to try harder."

She giggled again as her father approached, his arm still wrapped around his wife's shoulders. She gazed up at him with adoration in her big brown eyes, which were heavily fringed with dark lashes.

Quickly, Donovan made introductions.

"I'm so glad you could come," Bobbie exclaimed, her friendly expression settling a few of Kirby's butterflies. "We've all been dying to meet you."

Warmed by her enthusiasm, Kirby glanced down as Rose tugged on her jacket.

"You're my new aunt," she said importantly. "Aunt Ashley is my old aunt."

"Don't let *old* Ashley hear you say that," Donovan warned. "She might not appreciate the comparison."

As Kirby looked into Rose's face, the child's re-

semblance to Donovan hit hard. She had the trademark Buchanan cleft in her chin, golden blond hair
swirling past her shoulders and her mother's dark
eyes. Indeed, she was the image of Kirby's own childhood pictures, displayed on the family piano back in
Boise.

"You're right, sweetheart. I'm your aunt Kirby,
and you're my one and only niece." Kirby squatted
down, blinking away tears. She hadn't thought she'd
be so moved by the sight of her brother's child. Now,
looking at Rose made her realize how much she had
missed out on over the last quarter century—time that
could never be recaptured. For a moment, bitterness
welled up in her throat, threatening to choke her.

"Come on, let's all go inside where it's warmer,"
Bobbie invited, wrapping the sides of her open jacket
tighter around her slim body. "I'm sure you'd like to
get settled in before supper."

Nodding, Kirby straightened. She intended to get
her luggage from the trunk. When she glanced
around, J.D. was waiting on the deck by the back
door, suitcases in hand. Wordlessly, he stepped aside
and then followed the rest of them into the house.
Kirby had the sensation he was holding himself separate from them, as though he were standing on the
other side of an invisible wall.

Donovan carried the other two bags. "Let's dump
these at the bottom of the stairs for now," he told
J.D. when they were all in the kitchen. "I'll take them
up later."

As the two men clumped down the hall, Kirby
looked around the large country kitchen, at the oak
cupboards, the counter tiled in a soft gray-green and
the massive six-burner stove. The window over the

sink was diamond paned and topped by a ruffled curtain in a cream-and-green print.

When J.D. followed Donovan back into the kitchen, Kirby took a deep breath. "It was nice to meet you," she said. "Thanks for coming to the airport." She hoped J.D. understood that she was thanking him for that brief moment of shared understanding as well.

Surprise flared briefly in his eyes and then he blinked it away. "No problem."

"Yeah, thanks, J.D.," Donovan added, clapping him on the back.

He stiffened visibly, and Kirby wondered whether her brother noticed. If he did, he ignored it. "I'll be down to the stable to check on Fanfare in a little while," he added instead. "Will you be around?"

"Sure thing, boss."

Kirby noticed the slight narrowing of Donovan's eyes, but J.D. was looking at her, not her brother. The intensity of his gaze beneath the brim of his hat sent a shiver of reaction sliding down her spine, even as she tried to convince herself he was only wondering whether she was still uncomfortable. Her smile of reassurance wavered when his own expression remained impassive.

"I'll send along some stew and cornbread for your supper," Bobbie told him.

J.D.'s expression softened slightly. "Much obliged." Touching two fingers to his hat brim, he sidestepped Kirby and left. With his departure, some of the energy seemed to leak from the kitchen.

"Come on," Bobbie said, breaking into Kirby's thoughts as she gave her shoulder a friendly squeeze. "Rose and I will show you to your room." Donovan tagged behind them up the carpeted stairs, toting her bags.

The first thing Kirby spotted in the cozy bedroom was a crystal vase full of fresh chrysanthemums sitting on the dresser. The sight of the cheery yellow and orange flowers reminded her of her mother's garden back in Boise, bringing with it an ache in her chest.

How could the Wilsons have kept the truth from her for all these years?

"Is this okay?" Bobbie asked with a worried glance around.

Realizing that something of her mixed feelings must show on her face, Kirby turned in a slow circle. "It's perfect. I'm really glad to be here." When she said the words, she realized how true they were. She'd been foolish to be nervous. These people were family. *Her* family.

Deliberately, Kirby admired the bed with its bright scrap quilt and polished maple headboard, the tall dresser, brass drawer pulls gleaming softly, and the matching desk. "I want to thank you for making me so welcome," she said softly.

Immediately, Bobbie gave her a quick hug. "I should be thanking you for making my husband so happy," she said after she had dropped her arms again. She glanced up at the tall blond who had just set Kirby's bags on the bed. "You have no idea how hard he prayed to find you. He never gave up."

Donovan gave his wife a smile edged with sweetness.

"Well," Bobbie exclaimed briskly, as if for a timeless moment he'd made her forget there was anyone else in the room, "just treat this as you would your own home, and let me know if there's anything else you need, okay?''

Deeply moved, Kirby thanked her again.

Bobbie straightened one of the eyelet window curtains that framed a plain white shade. "We thought we'd go over to Taylor's tomorrow after you've had time to catch your breath. I know he's eager to meet you, too."

Despite her resolution, Kirby felt a rush of fresh apprehension. She had talked to Taylor on the phone from Boise. Perhaps it was silly to worry about meeting her own brother, but he was eight years older than her and his face looked so serious in the snapshot Donovan had shown her.

Taylor's ranch was twenty miles away—a ranch he, too, had bought with prize money earned in the rodeo arena, wrestling steers instead of riding wild bulls.

She told herself to quit worrying about him. When had she grown so anxious about other people's opinions? Not when she'd decided to become a nurse instead of going to business school as her parents wanted. Not when she had encouraged her adopted brother, Jonathan, to remain true to himself despite what other people might say about him, and not when she had gotten fed up and walked out on her husband, a man her mother thought Kirby was lucky to have snared in the first place.

Squaring her shoulders, she returned Bobbie's smile. "I'm looking forward to meeting my other brother and his family."

"I promised I'd give him a call when we got here," Donovan said from the doorway. "You can say hi if you want."

"Of course I do. I'll be right down."

"Take your time. I've got some ranch business to discuss with him, too."

After Donovan had left the room, Kirby joined Bobbie at the window and looked out into the gathering darkness. It wasn't her oldest brother she pictured, though, as she stared through the glass. It was the image of the black-haired cowboy she had already met who danced before her mind's eye—enigmatic J. D. Reese.

Chapter Two

She already fit right in as if she'd been born here, J.D. thought as he walked the few hundred yards down the road to his own small house. He had never really fit in anywhere, even on the reservation, and the only person who'd ever believed in him was his mother.

He wasn't jealous of Kirby's instant acceptance into her brother's family, though. A woman needed people around her, but a loner like J.D. needed no one.

Snake, the stray dog he'd found out on the range, injured and starved, growled from his lair beneath the porch. Clearly the one-eyed mongrel felt as out of place on Buchanan land as J.D. did. The dog, who refused to set foot in the house or to let anyone near him, was just a damn sight more open about it.

"Easy, boy. It's only me."

Immediately the low-pitched growling stopped. One unblinking gold eye stared from the darkness under the porch, but the dog didn't venture out. Knowing any overture he made would be rejected, J.D. picked up Snake's empty food dish and went up the steps of the small, two-story house.

In the remodeled kitchen, J.D. dumped a can of dog food into Snake's dish. Setting it down outside, he went back in and shut the door. The dog wouldn't eat while anyone was hanging around.

J.D. pulled a soda from the fridge. He took a long drink, his mouth curving into a reluctant smile as he remembered comparing Kirby to little Rose. As soon as he realized what he was doing, his fingers tightened on the soda can and he headed for the stairs that led to the two bedrooms on the second floor. Perhaps a little hard work would wipe the woman's enticing image from his obviously fevered brain.

He'd been alone too long, he thought, and then he reminded himself that he liked it that way. Only sometimes, like tonight, it was damned hard to remember why.

His body was confusing need with lust, that was all. He hadn't been with a woman since before his accident, nearly a year ago. For a long time he had thought his libido had been smashed along with his hip. While he'd stayed at the reservation, letting his battered body mend, he just hadn't given a damn. About women, about anything. Perhaps part of his lethargy had been because of his mother's death from emphysema the year before. Since he'd come to Colorado, he rarely left the ranch.

Maybe he'd drive in to Caulder Springs or even up to Sterling this weekend and check out the action there. A couple of the men who worked Buchanan cattle, former rodeo riders like himself, hit the bars every Friday night. They'd stopped inviting him along, but he could always hitch a ride. Or he could go alone; he had his own wheels.

J.D. opened the door to the spare bedroom that he used as a shop and went inside. The sharp, familiar scent of raw wood greeted him like an old friend. On the workbench he'd nailed together from scrap lumber lay the partly completed lid for his current project, an oak chest with the image of a bareback bronc carved into the top. Next to it were several hand tools and a small belt sander.

J.D. crossed the room, his boots echoing on the bare floor, and ran his fingers lightly down the side of the chest, tracing the grain. Inhaling, he savored the pungent aroma of the cedar he had used to line it. His hand lingered on the raised design of the lid as he glanced around the familiar room.

A broom and a dustpan rested in one corner. Scraps of leftover hardwood were stacked against the wall. An old set of shelves held a small collection of books on furniture making and wood carving he had picked up at various used bookstores along the rodeo circuit.

With the help of those books and advice from an aging bullfighter, J.D. had taught himself to carve. His first projects had been tiny animals he'd whittled while he was waiting his turn in the chutes. Surprised at how easily shaping the wood came to him, he'd gone on to bigger challenges as soon as he'd gotten this workshop set up. With part of each paycheck, he'd bought more tools and pricier lumber. He had progressed to small boxes, then bigger chests, a low table, even the front door for Buchanan's new house.

On the outside panel, J.D. had carved several scenes of bucking bulls surrounded by a border of flowering vines.

Remembering his boss's astonishment at the gift, J.D. shifted uneasily. When he had given it to them, Bobbie had carried on as if it were fashioned from gold-inlaid mahogany rather than plain old oak. Without his knowledge, she had persuaded a friend of hers who owned a gift shop in Sterling to take two of his carved boxes on consignment. When they sold, the woman came to the ranch and talked him out of an ornate jewelry box lined in velvet, a set of carved wall plaques and another hope chest with an abstract design worked into the lid. To J.D.'s surprise, they, too, sold quickly. Now the woman was hounding him for more pieces.

Reaching up to a shelf above the bench, he switched on a small radio, filling the room with an old Hank Williams ballad. Then he picked up a tiny chisel and began detailing the bronco's tail. The subtle tension that had hummed through him all afternoon started fading. The faint throbbing in his temple slowed. He dragged in a deep breath and the knots in his shoulders worked loose. In moments, his attention was riveted on the design he was etching into the wood.

"Taylor, it's so nice to finally see you." Gazing up at her older brother, who had insisted on coming over "just for a minute" as soon as Donovan called him, Kirby was caught off guard by the flood of tears she had to blink away.

Taylor's dark gray eyes glittered suspiciously as well, despite his crooked grin. He was a big man, brown haired and built along more solid lines than Donovan. Seeing Taylor now, Kirby had a momentary recollection of a boy with the same serious gray eyes, the same crooked smile. Before she could focus on it, the hazy image faded.

"I've missed you, honey," he said, voice rough with emotion. The sound of that same voice, only younger and not so deep, echoed in the distant reaches of her mind.

"I remember you," she exclaimed. "When I fell in the gravel behind our trailer and skinned my knee, you put a striped bandage on it and told me not to cry."

Abruptly Taylor's smile faded and he went pale beneath his tan. His big hand shook as he reached out to touch her cheek with his fingertips.

"I remember that day," he said hoarsely. "You were wearing a pretty little blue dress Mama made for you. You got the skirt dirty when you fell." The muscles of his throat worked and then he swept Kirby into his arms, folding her in a bear hug that threatened to crack her ribs.

"Now, bro, don't go and break her when we just got her back," Donovan teased.

Kirby felt a shudder go through Taylor as he held her. All her worries about seeing him again melted away as she struggled with a fresh wave of emotion.

"I'm not gonna break her," he mumbled into her hair before he dropped his arms and let her suck in a breath to replace the one he had squeezed out of her with his hug.

"Honey, can you remember anything else?" Donovan demanded, searching her face as Taylor hovered protectively. "Anything about me? I used to let you play with my toy cars. We made roads in the dirt and had races.''

Dredging her mind for another snippet of memory, Kirby was finally forced to shake her head with reluctance. "I was only four. If I did remember you, I probably thought you were kids from the neighborhood. I'm sorry.''

Donovan shrugged. "That's okay. It's only natural that we remember more than you, being older.''

Before Kirby could think of anything else to say, Rose spoke up.

"Daddy told Mommy that Aunt Kirby used to look just like me," she informed Taylor. "Then J.D. said Daddy would have to shoot somebody.''

As Taylor's dark eyebrows rose in silent query, Kirby colored at the innocent reminder. Donovan laughed and put his hand on Rose's head. "That's not quite the way I explained it to Mommy.'' He glanced at Taylor. "He made some reference to my keeping a shotgun handy if Rose grew up to look like Kirby does now.''

Kirby's blush deepened as both brothers eyed her with interest.

"Sounds like you've got a fan," Taylor drawled, a teasing light in his eyes. "I didn't think Reese was big on compliments.''

"You're embarrassing her," Bobbie scolded. "And J.D. is a perfectly nice man.''

"I didn't say he wasn't," Taylor protested. "I just didn't think he chased the ladies.''

"And he'd better not start now, or I might need that shotgun sooner than I thought.'' Idly, Donovan smoothed his mustache with one finger, a speculative gleam in his eyes.

Kirby wished they'd drop the subject of the hired hand. Thinking about him made her curiously uncomfortable. "I don't think Mr. Reese likes women very much."

Taylor hooted with laughter. "Honey, he's a cowboy. Next to their favorite horse, all cowboys like women. Some of them just aren't sure what to do about it."

Bobbie gave him a playful push. "If Ashley heard you talking about horses like that, you might end up sharing a stall with yours," she scolded.

"We were talking about Kirby and J.D.," Donovan reminded her.

"There *is* no Kirby and J.D.," Kirby exclaimed. "I'm here to visit you. That's all." To her own ears, her protest sounded too strong. They were only teasing—just as she suspected they'd teased her when they were all children.

"That's okay, sis." Donovan's tone was reassuring. "J.D.'s a loner. He won't bother you. If a female doesn't have four hooves and a mane, he's not interested."

Kirby wasn't so sure that J.D.'s attention would have been a bother. Despite his unfriendly attitude, there was something about him that she found attractive—something she shied away from examining too closely, since she definitely wasn't in the market for a fling with a cowboy.

"So how's my favorite niece?" Taylor asked, changing the subject by scooping Rose into his powerful arms.

Relieved to be out of the spotlight, at least temporarily, Kirby watched him blow noisily on Rose's neck, making her giggle with delight. He'd shed the heavy plaid jacket he'd been wearing, but he still had on a baseball cap with a Broncos logo, a Western shirt with pearl snaps and jeans.

"I'm fine and dandy," Rose replied, leaning back in his arms. "Tell us the story of how Daddy found Aunt Kirby again."

Taylor gave Kirby a broad wink. "What story is that?" he asked Rose with a straight face.

She rolled her brown eyes expressively. "Uncle Taylor! You know. How the bareback bronc rider told Daddy he ran into a lady who looked just like him when he went to the doctor to fix his busted arm."

"Don't say busted," Bobbie interjected. "The man's arm was broken."

"The lady looked like the bronc rider?" Taylor asked.

Rose thumped his broad chest with her hand. "No, no, no. She looked like my daddy, only lots prettier."

"Oh, I remember that part," Taylor replied with an unabashed grin.

"You would," Donovan said.

"Well, I'll admit that hardly anyone's prettier than your dad, with all that yellow hair and that cute little dimple in his chin, but I think Aunt Kirby's just about got him beat in the looks department," Taylor drawled, giving her a teasing glance over Rose's head.

Before Kirby could protest, the wall phone rang. Donovan lifted the receiver.

"Yeah, I'll be right there," he said, after listening for a moment. He hung up and glanced at Taylor. "That was Reese. I told him I'd be down to look at Fanfare, my new broodmare, and he's getting antsy."

"I don't know why you put up with his attitude," Taylor groused.

"Yeah, you do."

It appeared to Kirby that Donovan's expression carried a silent warning. The exchange whetted her curiosity about the horse trainer. First chance she got, she'd ask Donovan what his cryptic comment meant.

"I'll come with you," Taylor offered, setting Rose on her feet. "I want to see this wonder horse you've been bragging about."

"Would you take J.D.'s stew down with you?" Bobbie asked. "It's all ready to go."

Donovan picked up the small pot from the counter. "You spoil him."

"Can you blame me?" she asked quietly.

He didn't answer, and Kirby's curiosity was stirred again. "Can I come, too?" she asked.

"If you aren't too tired," Donovan replied. "She'll keep for another day, you know." Yet he appeared so pleased by her interest that Kirby felt guilty.

Not guilty enough, though, to admit that it was the horse *trainer* who intrigued her and not her brother's leopard-spotted mare.

As J.D. stood in Fanfare's stall and watched her eat, he stroked the mare's neck as lovingly as he'd stroked the fine grain of the oak chest earlier. For a little while he had gotten so absorbed in its design that he'd almost forgotten he was supposed to meet his boss at the stable. While he waited for Buchanan, he double-checked the pregnant mare. She seemed to be settling in at her new home with no ill effects from her recent trip from Texas.

"Just don't run me into the wall with your butt

again and we'll get along fine," he murmured to her when his hip twinged sharply.

The mare's ears swiveled in the direction of his voice, but she didn't stop eating. Even a horse had priorities, and a bothersome human had to be way down the list—well past food and water.

He gave her rounded side a last affectionate pat and was about to let himself out of her stall when he heard the stable door open. The sound of feminine laughter made him tense up; it wasn't Mrs. Buchanan's familiar voice that floated toward him but the boss's new kin.

Turning slowly, he looked at both men before he allowed his gaze to settle on the woman with them. Was that answering awareness he saw in her eyes, or just simple interest in her surroundings?

"Let's see this new broom tail my bro's been braggin' on," Taylor drawled with a conspiratorial wink. "You'd think it was the first hoss he'd ever seen with four legs."

"She's better than anything you've got on that patch of scrub you call a ranch," J.D. replied mildly.

His boss's crack of laughter almost made him smile. Sometimes the brothers' sparring amused him; at other times it only made him feel more alone.

J.D. was aware of Kirby's gaze on him, but he took his time meeting it. She had the kind of expressive face that made her feelings easy to read, and she appeared amused by his remark.

He kept his own face blank. When the light faded from her eyes he felt a twinge of remorse, but then his deep-seated survival instinct kicked in. Maintaining a barrier between them was imperative, despite the temptation to flirt with her and irritate his boss.

He knew it in his gut as surely as he knew his hip was held together with plates and pins.

"Here's Bobbie's stew and a chunk of cornbread." Donovan set down a covered pot on a nearby table.

"Thank her for me." J.D. stepped out of the stall and leaned down to lift the lid off the kettle, but it wasn't the savory smell of the stew that made his mouth water. Damn, but he'd better get to town before he lost his head altogether and ended up testing not only the extent of Buchanan's tolerance, but his own self-control as well.

How would Kirby Wilson handle a pass from a ranch hand? Would she freeze him out? Try to let him down gently? Run to her brother? Was there a chance she'd be interested?

The idea had him smothering a wry chuckle. Not that he'd turn down an opportunity to find out if her lips were as soft as they looked, but he was a has-been rodeo bum, not a hotshot bull rider. His days of attracting a woman like her had been over since he'd jumped in the path of a speeding pickup truck.

The lid of the stew pot slipped from his fingers and clattered against the table, making Kirby stare and Fanfare nicker with alarm.

"Easy, girl." Donovan went into the stall to quiet the spooked mare as J.D. covered the pot and silently cursed his sudden clumsiness.

Nerves still jumping from the commotion, Kirby took a deep breath and peered through the vertical bars that filled the top half of the stall door.

This close, the horse looked huge. It was white with small black spots, reminding Kirby more of a Dalmatian than a leopard. When Donovan ran a hand over its wide back, the animal turned its head to regard him with one large eye as it snuffled his arm. Even Kirby could tell that he handled the horse with the easy expertise of someone who had been around them all his life.

"How's she doing?" he asked J.D., running his hands down each of its legs and picking up its hooves in turn. Then he straightened and stroked the horse's bulging stomach.

"You'd think she'd been born here." J.D. stuck a toothpick in the corner of his mouth and lounged in the entrance to the stall.

Kirby tried without success to ignore the width of his shoulders, straining against the soft flannel of his shirt, and the way his worn jeans fit his compact hips.

Taylor was standing next to J.D. "Give me a nice brown quarter horse," he mused as he rubbed one dark sideburn with his finger. "Don't you think all those spots are kind of distracting?"

Kirby was getting used to the continuous byplay between her brothers, but she couldn't help wondering what J.D. thought. He watched them silently, a part of the group and yet somehow separate from the rest of them.

"If you'll close up here when you're done," he said, taking a step back and almost bumping into Kirby before she moved hastily away, "I think I'll go heat up my dinner."

Donovan glanced up as if he had forgotten all about J.D.'s presence. "Sure thing," he said. "I'll see you in the morning before I ride out."

Taylor tipped his head. "Catch you later, J.D."

The trainer caught Kirby's eye as he reached for the pot of stew. Had he noticed how quickly she'd skittered away from him? Had it offended him? Not that *he* seemed to care if *she* took offense from his attitude.

"Enjoy your meal," she said lightly.

His expression sharpened. "Thanks. I intend to."

The next day a chill wind blew in, sucking the color from the sky and turning it pale and dismal as the temperature plunged. Exhausted, Kirby slept late. When she finally opened her door, the mouthwatering aroma of freshly baked bread greeted her. Wandering downstairs, she worried that she'd inconvenienced Bobbie by her belated appearance. Following her nose, Kirby found her sister-in-law in the kitchen with Rose.

"You're just in time to help taste test our first batch," Bobbie said, cutting slices off a golden loaf with a serrated knife after she had brushed aside Kirby's apology. "There's coffee if you'd like a cup."

While Rose explained that they were trying out a new recipe for cinnamon bread, Kirby helped herself.

"It smells heavenly." She inhaled deeply. In moments, the three of them were seated at the table eating warm slices of the fresh bread topped with melted butter.

"Not bad," Bobbie said before Kirby could tell her how delicious it was. "Honey, what do you think?"

Rose's head bobbed, making her golden curls dance. "I like it more than the old kind. Can I take some to J.D.?"

Bobbie glanced at the counter, where another loaf rested on a wire rack. "As soon as it's cool," she replied.

At her urging, Kirby helped herself to a second

slice. "It's wonderful." Before she could say anything more, Donovan came through the back door. As Bobbie pushed back her chair and got to her feet, he inhaled deeply.

"Sweetheart, I love your new perfume," he teased.

Buttering two slices and pressing them together, she handed him the makeshift sandwich. After he'd sampled it and expressed his approval, he went upstairs to shower and change for their visit to Taylor's.

When Bobbie sat back down at the table, Kirby noticed that she was smiling softly. Obviously, she and Donovan were deeply in love, even though he had confided to Kirby that he'd left her shortly after they first met, and that he hadn't known about Rose until she was four.

Over dinner at Taylor's later, Kirby could see that Taylor, too, had been lucky in love. His wife, a retired barrel racer he'd met on the rodeo circuit, was a pretty woman with wavy, red-gold hair. Like Bobbie, she put Kirby instantly at ease with her warm and friendly manner. Taylor beamed whenever he looked at her, his solemn expression softening into one of quiet happiness.

By the time Kirby headed back to the Rocking Rose early that evening with Donovan's family, the wind had finally died down, but the temperature was still dropping. It had been cold enough that afternoon, so she'd been grateful when Taylor suggested postponing the outdoor tour he'd planned.

"Ashley's nice," she volunteered from the back seat of the sedan she shared with her young niece.

"She's been good for the bro," Donovan replied. "Being married has loosened him up."

Kirby dredged for shared childhood memories, but

all she met with was a blank. It had been too long ago. Frustrated, she blinked back tears, vowing to get as much from this visit as she possibly could. "The boys are terrific," she ventured, remembering how like their father his three sons were in appearance, how unlike him they seemed in temperament.

"The boys are little terrors," Donovan corrected her dryly as he turned onto the ranch road. "Serves Taylor right for being so bossy when we were kids."

Kirby was about to reply when she saw headlights approaching them on the narrow dirt road. Donovan pulled the car over as far as he could and rolled down his window, as did the other driver, whom she recognized as J.D. Surreptitiously, she smoothed a hand over her hair.

"Everything okay?" Donovan asked him.

In the dim light, Kirby could see that J.D.'s hair hung loose beneath his black cowboy hat and that it brushed his shoulders, giving him an untamed appearance. Briefly, his hooded gaze flicked around the car, not quite meeting hers. "Ladies," he said, nodding.

"Hi, J.D.," Rose shouted from the far side of the back seat. Kirby's lips curved politely, but he'd already returned his attention to her brother.

"The horses are all tucked in," he said shortly, "and I've got business in town. I'll check on them again after I get back."

"Can I go with you?" Rose asked.

Before he could answer, Bobbie said, "Not this time, honey, Tomorrow's a school day and you need a bath."

With a noisy sigh, Rose thumped back against the seat, shoulders slumped with obvious disappointment.

"Perhaps I'll see you tomorrow after school," J.D. suggested, bringing the smile back to her face.

"Okay." Her small body had miraculously lost its droop. Studying her niece, Kirby thought wryly that she understood Rose's excitement. If he'd said that to *her,* she would have responded the same way.

"See you in the morning, then," Donovan told him, closing the window.

J.D.'s truck was already moving again and his gaze was focused straight ahead. Kirby couldn't help but notice how classically handsome his profile was as she watched him go by. If she wasn't careful, someone would catch her gaping at him like an adolescent mooning over the current teen idol.

Shifting her gaze, she caught Donovan's reflection in the rearview mirror and realized he'd been watching her. A blush swept up her cheeks, but to her relief, he didn't comment.

"I'm surprised he'd go into town on a weeknight," he said instead. "That's not like J.D."

"Maybe he's met someone," Bobbie replied.

Donovan gave her a questioning look.

"A woman," she elaborated. "Perhaps the man has a girlfriend."

Kirby felt a sudden pain in her chest, surprising in its intensity. Whether J. D. Reese had a girlfriend or not was no concern of hers. She hardly knew him. So why was she relieved to hear her brother's comment that, as far as he knew, J.D. hadn't been to town in at least two months?

"How are you settling in?" Donovan asked Kirby the next evening as she sat across from him in his cluttered office down the hall from the kitchen. She'd never been in here before, but when Bobbie had showed Kirby around the house this morning she'd referred to it as the last bastion of his shrinking domain. "Is there anything you need? Anything I can do to make your visit better?"

Kirby shook her head. "I'm fine," she said, ignoring the little prickle of apprehension she'd felt when he asked her to come into the office with him. "Everyone has been wonderful, especially Bobbie, and your daughter is a sweetheart."

His expression softened at her comment. It was easy to see that he loved them both dearly. Kirby was happy for him, but his obvious contentment left her feeling strangely restless.

To give herself a few moments, she sank deeper into the chair's well-padded embrace and inhaled the faint scent of the leather. She looked around more carefully, first at the ancient wooden desk and then at the modern computer sitting incongruously on its satiny surface. Next to the monitor stood a small carving of an old, swaybacked horse, head hanging and ribs clearly delineated. The sorry little figure was so lifelike that Kirby found her heart aching at its implied neglect.

On the corner of the desk nearest her stood a cluster of photographs in brass frames. All but one were in full color, pictures of Rose and Bobbie. The photo that snagged her attention was black and white and bore a crease across one corner.

Curious, Kirby picked up the studio portrait, of a young couple wearing outdated clothing and hairstyles. The man had light hair and a cleft in his chin; the woman's eyes reminded Kirby of their older brother. Her heart began to thud with apprehension and she looked beseechingly at Donovan.

"Who are they?" she asked in a ragged whisper, but she already knew the answer.

"Our parents." His voice was gentle; his expression watchful. "Do you remember them?"

She gave a jerky shrug. "They look familiar." With a finger that trembled, she touched the glass protecting their images, sure she'd seen this picture before.

"Do you know where they are?" she asked. How old would they be? "Are they alive?"

Slowly, he shook his head as he took the picture from her unresisting grip and set it back on the desk. Then he enfolded both her hands in his much bigger ones.

"I'm sorry, honey, but they probably died the same night they disappeared, when you were only four."

Kirby tried to absorb his words, but she was too numb. Waiting for the disappointment to hit, she felt instead an emptiness that chilled her like a winter wind, making her shiver with dread. Vaguely, she realized he was chaffing her hands between his own, as if he could feel the coldness threatening to engulf her.

Something brushed against Kirby's cheek. Freeing one hand from his and reaching up, she was startled to feel the wetness of a tear on her fingertip. She had started crying without even realizing it.

Donovan pulled a tissue from a box on the desk and handed it to her silently. As she dabbed at her eyes, he looked away and cleared his throat. This must be even harder on him than it was on her, she realized. He'd been old enough to remember the last time he'd seen their parents alive.

"How did they die?" she asked baldly. Now that she knew of their existence, it didn't seem fair that she had no memories of her own.

For a long moment Donovan's gaze searched hers, as if he was deciding how much to tell her. Then he leaned back and with apparent nonchalance, rested one booted foot on his other knee. But the knuckles of the hand that gripped his ankle were white with strain.

"As far as we can tell, they died that night twenty-five years ago," he replied, his attention riveted on the old photograph. "They were going out for the evening. Their car plunged over a bank into a deep ravine and they were probably killed instantly."

"What do you mean, as far as you can tell?" Kirby asked resentfully. Why had she been separated from her brothers? Why hadn't they stayed in touch with her? "If you know they were in an accident, why don't you know when it happened? Where did you think they were?"

"Taylor and I finally learned the truth less than a year ago, when their bodies were discovered. Until then, we thought they'd deserted us on purpose."

"My God! How awful that must have been for you." Her shock must have shown on her face, because Donovan went on to explain that the wrecked car, hidden from sight by the undergrowth, had only recently been discovered by a firefighting crew.

"The police back in Idaho assured me they didn't suffer, waiting for a rescue that never came," he said, his voice vibrating with suppressed emotion. "And we know now that they never meant to leave us."

He turned his head away, and she realized how the boys must have felt, growing up wondering if their parents had abandoned them deliberately. Questions crowded her mind, demanding answers.

"Oh, honey," she murmured instead, touching his muscular arm. "Of course they didn't desert us. I'm truly sorry you ever thought that."

Abruptly, Donovan got to his feet. "At least now we know the truth," he said, his voice only slightly rough. He looked down at her, his somber expression easing slightly. "Perhaps I should have told you right away, but there was so much else for you to absorb. I didn't want to hit you with too much all at once."

Kirby got up, too, legs shaky. "I understand. Thank you for telling me now. It couldn't have been easy."

He shrugged. "Are you okay?"

She wasn't entirely sure. Perhaps it hadn't sunk in yet. Maybe it never really would. It wasn't as if she remembered her parents, not the way she knew the people who had raised her—the ones who'd lied to her. The bitter emotion she felt toward them was very real, and somehow it combined with her disappointment, threatening to swamp her shaky composure. She couldn't deal with that now.

Unexpected tears clogged her throat and burned her eyes.

"I'm all right," she murmured, trying to blink away the moisture as Donovan watched her anxiously.

"Are you sure?" He offered her another tissue. Seeing an answering sheen in his eyes, she struggled to keep her tears from spilling over. Giving in to the powerful sense of loss would only make him feel even worse.

"Yes, I'm sure." Her voice wobbled slightly. "I

only wish I'd been around when you first found out what happened to them.''

''Me, too.''

She didn't want to risk upsetting either of them further with more questions. Questions that could keep for now. Instead, she dredged up a smile that wobbled only slightly. ''Would it be okay if I took a walk?'' she asked. It was dark out, but the wind had died down. ''I think I need to be by myself for a little while.''

''Now?'' He looked startled, and then his expression softened with understanding. ''Of course you can. The stable is pretty deserted at this time of night,'' he added as he drew her into his arms for a gentle hug. ''It's warm and peaceful, and the horses never fail to calm me.''

For a few moments, Kirby took comfort in his brotherly embrace, until new tears threatened. If she didn't get out of here quickly, she was going to fall apart. And Donovan, being the kind of man he was, would suffer right along with her.

''Maybe I'll check it out,'' she told him as she stepped back.

''We'll talk again.''

He must understand that she had to absorb what he'd already told her before she could deal with any more. ''I'd like that,'' she said before she left. ''Thanks.''

Waving a flashlight ahead of her as she drank in the silence of the quiet night, Kirby made her way down the driveway. Despite the Buchanans' warm acceptance of her, she was grateful for the temporary solitude.

In the distance loomed the stable, illuminated by the glow from a tall utility light. Beyond it were other outbuildings she knew included a bunkhouse, a couple of hay sheds and an old barn where some of the equipment and ranch vehicles were stored.

Off to her left, a narrower road angled into the darkness. She felt more like walking than visiting the horses, but the last thing she wanted tonight was to run into some gregarious cowboys, even though she assumed they'd be nice enough to the boss's sister.

Indecisively, free hand buried in the pocket of her parka, she peered down each road in turn. Then she heard a burst of masculine laughter from the direction of the bunkhouse. A match flared in the darkness outside the circle of light, making her opt to explore the narrower path instead. Surely there was nowhere on the ranch where she could get into trouble, except perhaps the open range. In a few moments she would head back to the house, where Donovan no doubt waited anxiously to make sure the news he'd given her hadn't upset her too much.

Head bowed, Kirby picked her way slowly, following the beam of her flashlight. Rounding a curve in the darkness, she noticed a small, two-story house ahead in the gloom. The windows were dark; perhaps it was vacant.

She was about to walk past the building when she heard a low, rumbling growl from the direction of the porch. Freezing in place, she didn't even dare to lift the flashlight enough to see what was making the threatening noise.

Her blood turned cold as she wondered if the single yellow eye she saw reflecting the glow of her flashlight could be that of a coyote or a wolf. No doubt even a ranch dog would growl at a stranger, but would it attack her?

She managed one stumbling step backward, hoping for a prudent, if cowardly, retreat. At her slow, trembling movement, the growl increased in both volume and intensity.

"Nice boy," she called, her voice thinned by the fear clamping her throat shut. "Good dog." At least she hoped it was a dog.

The menacing sound continued. Her knees were shaking; the beam of the flashlight bounced up and down in time with her thundering heartbeat.

Just when Kirby was beginning to wonder if a person could truly die of fright, the front door of the little house burst open, the glow of habitation from inside as welcome as a whole team of animal-control officers.

"Snake, what the hell's the matter?" demanded a familiar voice. "You got a serial killer cornered out here? You're sure making a damned racket."

The porch light snapped on, nearly blinding Kirby, who was still frozen in place like a child playing statues. Squinting into the sudden brightness, she could barely make out the figure silhouetted in the doorway. At least the growling had stopped abruptly.

"It's just me," she squeaked. "Is that your dog?" Realizing how dumb her question must sound, she pressed her lips together and tried to steady the flashlight aimed at the ground in front of her.

"What are *you* doing here?" J.D.'s voice was filled with hostility.

The sudden mix of relief and embarrassment Kirby felt was too much for her already overloaded emotional state. Before she could turn her face away from his intense scrutiny in the glow from the light, the dam of her control crumbled and she humiliated herself even further by bursting into tears.

Chapter Three

Stunned, J.D. stared at the woman standing in the glow of the porch light, her blond head bowed. Her shoulders were hunched, making her appear small and vulnerable. Before she had spun away and buried her face in her hands, he'd seen that her eyes were awash with tears.

"What's wrong?" He hurried down the steps, his bad hip nearly sending him sprawling. Back at the airport, his first impression of Donovan's sister had been of a woman who didn't lose control easily. It was more than the mongrel dog that had her coming apart now; J.D. was sure of it.

"I'm sorry," Kirby gasped as he reached her. No doubt breaking down like this was something she hated doing—especially in front of a virtual stranger like him.

The light from the porch turned her hair to a golden

curtain, making his fingers itch to stroke it. Instead, he held his arms loosely at his sides, like a gunfighter waiting for his opponent to make the first move.

"It's okay, it's okay." He flexed his fingers. "The dog won't hurt you. He's probably more scared of you than you are of him."

She raised her head and swiped at her wet cheeks while he pretended not to notice. "I doubt that."

"Maybe not," he muttered, wishing he knew better how to offer comfort. "But you're pretty scary, city girl."

Her eyes widened in disbelief. "You don't look like a man who—who's afraid of anything."

The hitch in her voice jolted him as much as her words did. Remembering his impression that she could be more trouble than he needed, he said dryly, "I've got an instinct for self-preservation."

She frowned and tipped her head to one side as she scrutinized him intently through eyes that were silvery green and still shimmering with moisture. He knew only too well what she saw when she looked at him, and it wasn't the kind of man she was undoubtedly used to. How could he hope to hold the interest of a woman like her?

The thought pulled him up short. Why the hell would he want to?

In the cold light, a solitary tear clung to her long, curling lashes, making him wonder how she would react if he caught that glistening drop with his finger. "What are you doing out here in the dark?" His voice came out rougher than he'd intended.

"I needed some air, so I took a walk."

"I'm surprised your brother would let you loose by yourself." J.D. pictured Buchanan as pretty damned protective when it came to his family. It was easy to see they meant the world to him.

"I'm a grown woman," Kirby exclaimed.

J.D. had noticed precisely how much woman she was. Before he could think of something to say, her chin rose fractionally. Her full mouth trembled before she managed to firm it and something tightened inside him, followed by a wave of self-disgust.

What kind of bastard would think of tasting those soft lips when something was so obviously bothering her?

"I'm sorry that I overreacted, but your dog caught me by surprise," she said softly. "I'm not normally such a ninny."

Her smile, still shaky at the corners, sliced into him like the blade of a skinning knife. He longed to touch her, but he wasn't sure it was comfort he'd be offering.

"No problem." He wasn't about to tell her he suspected there was more to her distress than she was willing to admit. "Snake can be pretty intimidating, especially when it's dark and you don't know what you're dealing with." It was a long speech for him. Abruptly he stopped, wishing she'd turn around and head back the way she'd come. Wishing he still smoked, so he could busy himself with lighting a cigarette.

What was she doing, wandering around outside his house? He could be the kind of man who'd grab first and ask permission later, if at all, and then where would she be? Buchanan ran a tight ship, but some men reacted badly to temptation—and Kirby was as tempting as ice cream on a hot day.

J.D. realized she mustn't yet be all that familiar

with the layout of the ranch or she probably wouldn't have come this way. The only thing on this road before it merged again with the other one was his house.

Or was she playing at something?

He dismissed the thought as soon as it took shape. He'd had his share of women when he'd been winning, but he had no ego when it came to knowing what the main attraction had been. Pockets full of money were a powerful aphrodisiac, but his pockets were as flat as a deflated balloon these days and his rodeo buckles had started to tarnish. Besides, her brother had money, if that was what she wanted.

It was obvious that J.D.'s silent perusal made her uncomfortable. "I'm sorry I bothered you," she said again, glancing around. Snake had retreated to his lair beneath the porch, but J.D. had no doubt that the dog was still watching them warily. It trusted no one.

As Kirby clutched her jacket tighter, a gust of wind caught at her hair and made her shiver. J.D. felt a sudden, unexpected attack of conscience. "Uh, would you like some coffee?" The invitation tumbled out before he could stop it.

A tiny frown pinched the skin between her delicate brows. "Coffee?" she echoed.

He couldn't help but grin. "Yeah, that brown stuff. I've heard that it actually comes from beans they grow in Brazil."

Her lips curved at his teasing. "No kidding? They make it from beans?"

He was about to make another flippant remark when he realized what he was doing and damned near swallowed his tongue to keep from prolonging the ridiculous exchange.

"It's hot and it's strong," he said instead. "I don't

bother with decaf and you look like you could use a shot of high-test.'' He hunched his shoulders defensively, prepared to make a hasty retreat, when she surprised him again.

''Thank you. A cup of coffee would be nice.''

Hell, he hadn't expected her to accept. Hadn't even known he was going to offer until the words came out of his mouth. Didn't the woman have a lick of sense?

Reluctantly he led the way up the steps, wishing Snake had succeeded in running her off even as J.D. tried to remember whether he'd picked up the living room earlier.

Kirby followed him slowly, still not convinced that the dog wouldn't leap from beneath the porch and rip out her throat. As she glanced back over her shoulder, she wondered which posed the greater danger, the beast or its master.

J.D. pushed the front door open wider and stepped aside politely. Wishing she could better read his face, backlit by the bare bulb over the door frame, Kirby walked directly into the small living room and looked around. It was sparsely furnished and scrupulously neat.

While she tried not to appear too nosy, J.D. brushed past her and headed into the kitchen. His boots thudded against the bare floor, the slight hitch to his gait barely discernible.

''I hope you take your coffee black.'' His tone was slightly defensive. ''I don't keep any milk on hand.''

''Black's fine.'' Perhaps she should have turned down the offer he'd no doubt made only because he felt obligated. Then she remembered his attitude toward Donovan. No, J.D. Reese wasn't a man who appeared to give much thought to the social niceties. So, if he wasn't trying to be polite or to curry favor with his employer, why had he bothered? Her curiosity was instantly aroused. Was it possible that her reluctant interest was returned in some small measure? But what would a fascinating cowboy like J.D. see in an ordinary nurse like herself?

"Thank you," she murmured, when he handed her a steaming mug. He didn't offer her a seat, she noticed—and his other hand was empty. "Aren't you having any?"

He shook his head. His expression was unreadable, his black eyes veiled by the sweep of his lashes, a thick fringe that did nothing to compromise the masculine strength of his face.

"What set you off?" he asked, gesturing toward the door as she shifted her attention to the full mug. Although the question itself was brusque, even rude, his tone was not. He sounded as if he might be genuinely interested.

Stalling, Kirby took a sip of her coffee and barely suppressed a shudder. It was strong and bitter.

She must have been unsuccessful in hiding her reaction, because the hard line of his mouth softened slightly.

"Too potent?" he asked.

Probably, she thought, bemused. "Not at all." Gamely, she took another deliberate sip. "It's just the way I like it."

"Didn't your mother teach you not to tell lies?" Now he did smile as he hooked his thumbs into his wide belt and shifted his weight, his Western buckle glowing dully.

The change in his expression made her breath hitch

in her throat and his assessing glance swept over her as she subdued the urge to smooth down her wind-blown hair with her free hand. Instead, she raised the mug again, watching him steadily.

"It was only a little white lie," she replied, when her breathing had returned to normal.

"I see. I guess that's all right."

He really was attractive, but she wasn't sure just why he appealed to her so strongly. His appearance was hardly textbook handsome. His eyes were as dark and opaque as the coffee he'd given her, his face had a burnished hue. The straightness of his nose was marred by a bump on its arrogant bridge and his mouth, even pressed into a firm line as it was now, caused a coil of unnamed longing to tighten within her.

Suddenly she felt less than safe with him, although she didn't worry for a moment that he would say or do anything remotely out of line. No, it was her own behavior that concerned her. If he even suspected that she found him attractive, she'd die of humiliation.

"I'd better get back," she said, looking around for somewhere to set down her mug. "I don't want my brother to worry about me." Abruptly, she remembered the sorrowful news that had sent her down here in the first place. If nothing else, her encounter with the horse trainer had distracted her from that for a little while.

Had her mention of her brother been deliberate? J.D. wondered—a less-than-subtle reminder of just who she was and her place in the pecking order around here, in case he was getting ideas above his station? Perversely, he shifted to block her exit from his house.

"You didn't tell me what upset you," he pressed, watching her eyes widen. He saw no fear there, only shadows. She wasn't weak, he guessed, despite her femininity. He wondered what had honed that inner strength. Disappointment? Heartache? Maybe the road she'd traveled hadn't been as easy as he'd assumed when he first saw her, wearing that subtle mantle of self assurance he associated with a life devoid of difficult choices.

She hesitated, and he figured she was going to ignore the question again. Then she cradled the half-full mug in her free hand and angled her head, managing to make him feel as if she were looking down at him despite the disparity in their heights. "Donovan just told me the parents I didn't know existed until recently actually died years ago," she said flatly. "It's strange—even though I don't remember them, the idea of never being able to meet them, to get to know them again, really hit me hard."

"I'm sorry," J.D. said automatically. "That must have been a shock."

"I didn't know that I was adopted when Donovan came to Boise. It's been a lot to take in." Her chest rose and fell on a sigh, riveting his attention.

Ruthlessly, he shoved aside the sudden urge to gather her close in a clumsy attempt at comfort. If he touched her, she'd slap him silly and rightly so, given the real direction of his thoughts.

His blood heated at the idea of holding her, and then his stomach clenched with the knowledge of what he'd want to do once he had her there. The idea shamed him, since he'd never forced his attentions on a woman and didn't intend to start now. What the hell had gotten into him, anyway?

If Kirby saw his sudden frown, she ignored it. "I'm still trying to adapt to all this," she admitted, making a sweeping gesture. "Two new brothers, this ranch, a family with nieces and nephews I had no idea existed. When Donnie told me our parents had been killed in an accident the night they disappeared—a night I can't even remember—it was nearly more than I could take in. I don't know why it upset me so much." She rubbed at her forehead with her fingers. "It's all been such a shock."

"I suppose it would be." J.D. didn't know what else to say, just knew he'd made unfair assumptions about her easy life. "They were still your parents, even if you don't remember them. Losing them has to hurt, no matter when it happened."

"You understand," she mused, making him flush with sharp, unexpected pleasure. "Perhaps it's as simple as that. They were still my parents. But how did you get to be so smart?"

"My mother died last year." He hadn't known he was going to tell her until he heard himself speak the words. "She had emphysema. Even though she'd been ill for a long time, it still hurt."

She was immediately sympathetic. "I'm sorry for your loss. Is your father still living?"

J.D. thought of the man he'd never known, the one who had abandoned J.D.'s mother before he had even been born and who'd obviously had no interest in a child of mixed blood.

He shrugged, impatient with himself for giving Kirby an opening in which to probe further into his life. "I have no idea if he's alive or dead."

If his reply made her more curious, she gave no sign of it as the silence stretched awkwardly between

them. "Well," she exclaimed, voice suddenly brisk.
"I've certainly taken up enough of your evening."
She shoved the mug at him. Automatically, his fingers
curled around it. "Thanks for the coffee, but now I'd
better get going before someone starts to worry." Her
gaze didn't quite meet his as she whirled and headed
for the door, leaving him to regret his unfriendliness.

Searching for some polite, meaningless response,
he came up empty. "I'll walk you back," he offered
instead.

Her smile was bright, brittle and as counterfeit as
a two-headed coin. "That's not necessary, but thanks.
I know the way now."

Watching her hesitate at the top of the steps, he
merely shrugged. "Suit yourself." He didn't bother
to add that he'd see her later, or that it had been nice
talking to her. He didn't like the idea of running into
her again—even though he knew she'd be impossible
to avoid—and tonight's visit hadn't been "nice."
Quite the opposite. She left him itchy and restless,
craving something he knew would only lead to more
trouble than he cared to deal with, even if the idea of
irritating her brother did appeal to him in a perverse
way.

She glanced over her shoulder, a question lurking
in her green cat's eyes. "Is it safe for me to leave?"
she asked. "I mean, will your dog pounce on me
when I do?"

J.D. was tempted to laugh, sure that he and Snake
were equally unwilling to claim each other. "Like I
told you, he's probably more scared of you than you
are of him." J.D. didn't add that perhaps *he* should
be wary of her as well, but he thought it as he cupped
her elbow and escorted her down the steps, wondering

if that could possibly be the warmth coming from her he felt through the sleeve of her heavy parka or if it was his own overheated thoughts tormenting him.

She had thanked him again for the coffee he suspected was even now eating a hole in her stomach, and he stood watching her retreat down the road to the main house, flashlight bobbing in front of her. Then he heard Snake's warning growl.

"Smart dog," J.D. muttered without glancing at the dark cave under the porch. "You just keep reminding me that she's trouble, in case I get dumb and forget."

"Hang on!"

Bundled up to her eyebrows against the recent drop in temperature as she bounced along in one of the ranch vehicles beside her brother, Kirby braced herself and continued looking around curiously.

Proud as a boy with a collection of baseball cards, Donovan had been showing her his herds of cattle. Now the two of them were headed in the direction of the main house, where Bobbie had promised homemade soup for lunch. After the chill of the morning, the idea of a hot meal was one Kirby looked forward to with enthusiasm.

Expertly, Donovan drove the Jeep down one of the unmarked dirt roads that seemed to crisscross the ranch. He had voiced his worry earlier that she would think the scenery less than appealing; instead she found that she loved the wide-open feel to the landscape, as if one could race all the way to the horizon and beyond without being impeded by anything more solid than a line of fence posts.

It had been a couple of days since her encounter

with J.D. and she hadn't seen him since. Nor had she mentioned the incident to Donovan, not wanting to alarm him or cause any problems for J.D. or his unfriendly dog. No doubt the animal had merely been acting on its protective instincts. It was nearly as wary as its master.

A shiver went through Kirby as she remembered those first few moments of blank terror before J.D. had come out of his house.

"Cold?" Donovan asked, glancing at her. His cheeks were red and his green eyes blazed with pride, making her glad she had accepted his uncharacteristically hesitant offer to take her with him this morning. "I could crank up the heater."

She shook her head. "Thanks, but I'm fine." Hot air already blasted her feet, and the thermal underwear Bobbie had loaned her that morning was more than adequate in keeping the rest of her warm.

Donovan's grin held glowing approval. "You come from hardy stock, my girl. I knew a little fresh air wouldn't get to you."

"Has J. D. Reese always had that limp?" she asked before she could lose her nerve. She'd been telling herself that his mood swings the other night hadn't impressed her, but he had apparently burrowed into her mind like a burr in a wool blanket. Even before then, ever since she'd intercepted that unspoken message between Donovan and Taylor, she'd wondered about the man.

Donovan steered the Jeep with one hand while he worried the ends of his mustache with the other. His gaze was fixed on the road ahead as if the deserted ribbon of dirt needed his complete attention. "A little over a year ago Reese was hit by a speeding truck."

Kirby gasped at the grisly image her brother's blunt words painted. She'd assumed he'd been injured in some kind of riding accident. "That's awful. How did it happen?"

"The truck was coming too fast through a parking lot, Rose stepped into its path and J.D. shoved her out of the way. I was too far away to do a damned thing, and if he'd hesitated, it would have been too late. As it was, he couldn't save himself."

Shocked, Kirby stared hard at her brother. The muscles along his jaw were bunched; no doubt talking about it was still difficult for him. "What a terrible thing to happen," she exclaimed. "Thank God he was there to save her."

"I'd only taken my eyes off her for a minute," Donovan replied, a wealth of bitterness in his voice. "I was talking to someone and she saw a friend of hers."

"Was she hurt?" Kirby asked, dismayed by the self-condemnation in Donovan's voice, but unsure what to say about it. Did he feel he was the one who should have been hit instead of J.D.?

"Rose was very lucky," her brother answered. "She escaped with a skinned knee from the gravel where he shoved her and a bad fright." When he glanced her way, his expression was edged with sadness. "Reese was a bull rider, second in the rankings right behind me, but he was the most naturally gifted one I've ever seen. He sacrificed his career to save my daughter." Donnie's voice had thickened with emotion.

Kirby's heart turned over when she realized how guilty he must feel. "You blame yourself."

Donovan raised one eyebrow. "Damned right I do.

If I'd been watching her, a man's career wouldn't have been destroyed in less than a second." He chewed his lip. "I was number one, but Reese was nipping at my heels. If he hadn't been injured, he might very well have passed me by, winning both the gold buckle and the endorsement contract that enabled me to buy this spread."

"You didn't do anything deliberately," Kirby protested. "It was an accident. And it was J.D.'s choice to save her."

Even before she finished speaking, Donovan was shaking his head. "No, honey, you don't understand. There was no time for choice. He reacted on a decent man's pure instinct—dealing with an accident that shouldn't have happened. It was his hair-trigger reaction time that saved her and cost him his career."

She pictured her smiling niece and trembled at the thought that little Rose might have been hurt, even killed, without J.D.'s intervention. Swallowing hard, Kirby wondered what his thoughts had been as he threw himself in the path of that speeding truck—or if he'd even had time to think.

Donovan stopped at a closed gate separating two pastures. "He refused to let me pay his medical bills and then, when the hospital released him, he disappeared. It took me months to track him down, two visits to Arizona before he'd even talk to me. Then I nearly had to hog-tie him and drag his butt back here by force to get him to come to work for me."

While Kirby was absorbing everything, Donovan swung out of the Jeep to open the gate. In a moment, he was back.

"This is no charity job," he continued gruffly as he drove through. His voice sounded defensive, as if this wasn't the first time he'd had to explain himself. "He's a damned good horse trainer."

Kirby scrambled from the Jeep before Donovan could move. "I'll close the gate." He'd already impressed on her how necessary that was as they drove between pastures and he pointed out the differences between the various groups of cattle. *Herds,* she reminded herself. She'd had no idea how he could tell them apart; the assorted bunches of brown, black and white cows all looked identical to her untrained eye.

"It was good of you to go after him," she said after she'd climbed back into the jeep. She knew from his search for her just how persistent her brother could be. "Not everyone would try to repay him after he'd rejected their first offer."

Donovan grunted noncommittally.

"Does his injury slow him down?" she asked, remembering the faint hitch to his stride.

"Not usually," Donovan replied. "He can sit a horse well enough, but the damage to his hip has kept him out of the arena."

Kirby had seen the way bull riders were tossed around, both at local rodeos back in Idaho and on television. Trying to picture either J.D. or Donovan clinging to the broad back of one of those huge, slobbering beasts made her insides tighten with dread. And then the irony of J.D.'s injury struck her. He had lived with so much danger and then he'd been hit in a parking lot.

"Do you think he misses competing?" she asked. "Do *you* miss it?"

"No, I don't," Donovan replied. "But I have Bobbie and Rose as well as this ranch. I was ready to quit, and I'm luckier than most." He sent her a warning glance. "I wouldn't bring this up around Reese, if I were you," he cautioned. "He's not talkative at the best of times, but the accident is an especially sore subject with him."

"I understand, but it's not as if J.D. and I chat a lot." She winced at her own defensive tone. "Or that I'd want to," she added hastily, realizing too late that she was only making things worse.

Donovan looked her way again, eyebrows lifted, as he steered the Jeep around a pothole in the road. "You may not know me well enough yet to want to accept my advice," he said, "but believe me when I tell you that Reese is a loner. He's not—"

Cheeks burning, Kirby interrupted. "Good heavens," she exclaimed, striving for a breezy tone, although part of her still ached over what fate and a speeding truck had done to J.D. "I hope you don't think I'm *interested* in Mr. Reese. I was just curious, that's all."

"There are a couple men I could introduce you to while you're here," Donovan offered after a few moments of shared silence. "One's a rancher like myself, never married, with a big spread, and the other is a vet who's been divorced for several years, no kids."

Kirby's burning cheeks felt as if they would spontaneously combust from the heat of sheer embarrassment. Did Donovan think he needed to find men for her? "If you're planning on doing any matchmaking while I'm here, I'll be on the next plane back to Boise, and that's a promise," she warned, only half jesting. "Don't forget that I went through a painful divorce myself a little over a year ago, so I'm in no hurry to jump back into that particular frying pan again anytime soon."

Donovan braked the Jeep and searched her face, forehead creased with worry. "You haven't sworn off marriage, have you?"

"What if I have?"

"Then I'd be sorry you felt that way."

His obvious concern made her relent. "I don't know yet how I feel," she admitted. "I just can't say I'd recommend the institution at this point in my life."

"Was it pretty bad?" he asked softly. "The divorce?"

She shrugged. Even though the love she thought she'd felt for Tim had died abruptly when he'd admitted to an affair with a co-worker, her disappointment still hurt. "I don't imagine ending a marriage is ever easy," she said quietly. "Getting over it takes time."

When Donovan covered her hand with his, she returned the squeeze he gave her. "I'm doing okay, though," she added. Narrowing her eyes deliberately, she shook a threatening finger at him. "But if you dare to so much as attempt to fix me up with any of your friends, I'll put barbed wire in your undershorts."

Donovan gave her a sheepish grin. "Okay, honey. It won't be easy, but I'll do what you ask."

Kirby breathed a silent sigh of relief. "Thanks."

"I can't speak for Bobbie, though," he added with a sly twinkle in his eye as he released the brake on the Jeep and they continued down the dirt road. "You might have to threaten her, too, and I don't know how she'd react to the idea of barbed wire in her drawers."

Kirby groaned aloud, nearly succeeding in drowning out his deep chuckle.

"I'll say one thing for Reese, though," he continued, "he's talented."

Grateful for the change of subject, Kirby was nonetheless reluctant to discuss the trainer further. Still, curiosity got the best of her. "You mean with the horses he trains?" she asked.

"That, too. But did you happen to notice that carving on the desk in my office? The one of the skinny little nag?"

Kirby remembered the tiny statue. The artist had captured the horse's neglected state so well that she'd actually felt sorry for the creature. "Yes, I did."

"That's one of Reese's," Donovan said, surprising her. "And he carved the front door of the house, too. He was offended when I offered to pay for it, said it was a housewarming present."

So the man's prickly hide was only a facade, Kirby thought with a little rush of pleasure. The door was beautiful, the rodeo scene on the outside as well done as anything she'd ever seen, and she'd meant to ask Donovan if it had been crafted by a local artist. The door was a perfect focal point to the outside of the lovely ranch house.

Now she thought of her adopted brother, Jon, and the exclusive furniture gallery he and his partner owned in Aspen. They charged a fortune for one-of-a-kind pieces and were always looking for something new to offer to the high-priced decorators and wealthy home owners who patronized their gallery.

"What's J.D. doing, wasting his time training horses?" she asked Donovan teasingly. "He could be making a fortune with his woodworking."

"I agree that he has talent," Donovan replied with a shrug, "but I don't know if a man could support himself that way. Bobbie sent a couple of his things to a shop in Sterling on consignment, but I haven't heard if they sold."

"If they're anything like what I've already seen, I'm sure someone snapped them up." Kirby was beginning to reassess her opinion of J.D. It would take someone with a tremendous degree of empathy to portray so poignantly the plight of the sad little equine figurine. Obviously, the man was more complex than she had first imagined.

"Just don't let his talent with wood or with horses blind you to his faults," Donovan said grimly as he accelerated, making Kirby wonder if he regretted telling her about the carving. "Despite what he did for my family, I don't know how far I'd trust him with my baby sister."

Her cheeks flamed anew. "I appreciate your concern," she said primly, "but when you know me better, you'll learn that I can take care of myself." J. D. Reese had No Trespassing signs all over him, and she wasn't a woman to disregard a warning that was so prominently posted.

Chapter Four

"You hired me to train your horses, not to baby-sit." J.D. knew he was being unfair, but he couldn't help himself. The boss's sister was getting under his skin and the last thing he needed was to spend more time around her. Thank the heavens she was going home to Idaho in a little over a week. It couldn't be soon enough for him.

Ignoring Buchanan, who was leaning against the railing, he led the yearling filly around in a tight circle in the indoor arena. The gray-and-white Appaloosa must have picked up on the annoyance in his tone; skittishly, she tossed her head.

J.D. lowered his voice to a husky whisper and murmured soothing words in an ancient language his maternal grandfather, Chee Whitehorse, had taught him as a boy.

Behind him, J.D. heard a dry chuckle that set his

teeth on edge. No matter how he attempted to bait Buchanan, the rancher ignored his jibes—and that drove J.D. crazy. Why couldn't the other man just once lose his temper and treat J.D. as he would any other employee who gave him a hard time?

The answer was obvious. Because he felt indebted.

It was a debt J.D. was sure Buchanan must resent every bit as much as J.D. did himself. Charity was charity, no matter how you sliced it. This job Buchanan had bullied him into accepting, the roof over his head, even the other man's steadfast refusal to fight back whenever J.D. unleashed his frustration— J.D. hadn't asked for any of it, and he damn well didn't want it.

But he hadn't been able to turn down the offer when Buchanan came a second time to the reservation where J.D. was holed up, licking his wounds from the accident and from his mother's death. His bull-riding career and the prize money he'd earned were gone, eaten up by his traveling expenses on the circuit and his mother's staggering medical bills, not to mention his own. He was the one who was indebted to Buchanan, and that ate at J.D. worst of all.

"What's so funny?" he couldn't keep from asking now.

"I doubt that most men would think of spending a few hours with my sister as baby-sitting," Buchanan drawled. "But she wants to learn to ride while she's here. I don't have the time to teach her myself, not with Rich leaving and Big Mike's arthritis bothering him so much."

J.D. grimaced at the mention of two more Buchanan charity cases—rodeo riders too old or stove up to compete any longer. "Okay, so she's not a bad-looking woman. She's still a greenhorn and I don't have the patience to deal with her," he growled, shoving the filly's head gently away when she crowded close to investigate the pocket of his shirt.

"Pretend Kirby's a horse," Buchanan suggested. "You seem to have patience enough for them."

Thinking of his boss's sister as anything other than the looker she was would have taken more imagination than J.D. possessed. An image of her the way she'd stepped out of the shadows the other night, all soft, trembling mouth and tear-drenched eyes, made his breath catch in his chest. Damn, but he didn't need that kind of temptation.

Apparently, Buchanan wasn't about to give up. "You taught Rose to ride. She was scared of horses until you showed up and she watched you working with the yearlings."

One more thing Buchanan probably thought he owed J.D. for. What could he say? It was true that he'd helped Rose over her fear. Ever since then, she'd been following him around like a bottle-fed calf. He didn't mind having her spend time with him, and apparently Buchanan didn't, either, even though J.D. had noticed she wasn't allowed to hang around the other cowhands unsupervised.

"I guess I could give your sister a few pointers," he conceded grudgingly, pretty sure he'd live to regret it. At least he could look at her, and hadn't someone once said that suffering built character? His character could use a little reconstruction.

"I appreciate your help." When Buchanan clapped him on the back, J.D. stiffened without thinking. Sometimes he'd envied the casual male camaraderie he'd seen around the rodeo chutes, but he'd never felt comfortable with it himself—perhaps because his own father had never been there when he was growing up. Except for his mother and a few buckle bunnies along the circuit, J.D. had been a loner for most of his life.

"Just don't complain if I get behind in my regular work," he cautioned sourly.

"Treat Kirby right and I won't complain about anything," Buchanan replied, resettling his Stetson as he turned to leave. "Besides, it will only be for a couple of days."

Treating Kirby right had about as much appeal to J.D. as did milking a rattlesnake. Either could get him in a seriously uncomfortable position if his attention wavered for a moment.

"How long has it been since you were on a horse, city girl?" Sitting with his booted feet propped on a storage trunk near the door to the tack room, J.D. didn't bother to glance up to where Kirby waited nervously for her first lesson. Instead he whittled meticulously at a small piece of wood. Shavings clung to the front of his green flannel shirt and a toothpick protruded from the corner of his mouth.

Since the previous afternoon, when she had accidentally overheard him telling her brother that he had no time for a greenhorn, Kirby had managed to convince herself she could at least do as well as her five-year-old niece. Now that the time had actually come for Kirby's first lesson, she wasn't so sure.

"I haven't been on a horse for years," she admitted, watching as the blade of his knife shaped the wood into a small bird, wings outspread.

"At least you had the sense to dress right."

Following the direction of his gaze, she glanced down at the jeans and the boots she wore with a thick blue sweater she had borrowed from Bobbie. She'd braided her hair into a fat rope, but already she could feel individual strands working loose to tickle her cheeks and neck. Her hand itched to tuck them back in, but she resisted the urge to fidget.

A horse in a nearby stall neighed softly and another replied as J.D. got to his feet, absently brushing the wood shavings from his clothes. Then he surprised her by holding out the tiny carving.

"It's a hawk," he said gruffly, while she studied the small object resting on his upraised hand. "You can have it if you want."

"Oh, thank you." When she picked up the tiny carving, her fingertips brushed his palm. Startled by the warmth of the fleeting contact, she glanced at his face. The expression in his dark eyes was unreadable, but a muscle twitched in his lean cheek. Confused, she examined the bird's delicate beak and the pattern of feathers etched into the light-colored wood.

Had he felt that lightning-quick sizzle of awareness as she had, or was she merely being silly about a figure straight out of an adolescent fantasy?

"This is beautiful," she murmured, as she touched the carving with care, awed by his talent.

Unable to regret his impulsive gesture, J.D. stared at her bent head as he did his best to ignore the way his palm still tingled from the brush of her fingers. "It's no big deal." He couldn't help it; her obvious entrancement pleased him more than the generous check he'd gotten from the gift shop in Sterling.

"I wish I had my purse," she murmured, glancing around. "I don't want it to get damaged or lost."

J.D. pulled a faded bandanna from his hip pocket. "Put it in this."

Handling the handkerchief, softened by many washings, as carefully as if it were the fanciest foil paper, she wrapped up the little hawk and tucked it into her shirt pocket. J.D. found himself envying a wooden bird, nestled snugly against her breast.

Aware of the direction of his gaze, Kirby searched for something to distract him.

"Is that my horse?" she asked, spotting the buckskin waiting in the arena, black tail swishing at a couple of flies. While she watched, nervousness growing, the mount shook its head, bridle jingling, and pawed the ground. Kirby had a sudden clear vision of herself sailing through the air over the horse's head to land in the dust at J.D.'s booted feet. So much for riding as well as Rose.

Obviously unconcerned, J.D. glanced at the buckskin and then back at Kirby, his lips twitching with amusement. "No, ma'am. That's my horse."

The tightness in her chest began to ease up. "Thank goodness."

"Wait here and I'll get Duke for you," he drawled, with a last pointed glance at the pocket in which she'd put the hawk.

Cheeks heating, Kirby watched him walk away down the aisle. Beneath the brim of his black Stetson, his hair was clubbed back into its usual neat ponytail. She remembered what it looked like hanging loose.

As if he could feel her bemused gaze, he swung around again, brows arched, and walked backward. "Not nervous, are you?"

"Me? Nervous about what?" Did the attraction she

felt toward him *show?* Had he given her the little bird because he found her interest amusing?

He spread his hands wide. "Nervous about getting on a horse. What did you think I meant?"

"I knew what you meant. I'm doing just fine." Kirby sent him what she hoped was a confident smile and linked the fingers of both hands together in front of her. "I'm looking forward to this."

His mouth curved into a grin that was downright sinful. "Didn't your mama teach you not to lie? First my coffee and now this."

The teasing tone, so unexpected, left her gaping. Lordy, what a smile did to his face!

"No matter," he said when she didn't reply. "I'll get your horse. Don't worry. He's nothing like Buck."

While she debated whether that was good or bad, picturing a broken-down plug that resembled the tiny statue on her brother's desk, she heard the door of a nearby stall slide open and then the low murmur of J.D.'s voice. Curious, Kirby followed him down the row.

She stopped when she saw him lead a huge black horse into the aisle. Duke looked neither broken-down nor neglected as he swung his head around to look at her through brown eyes glowing with intelligence.

Cross-tying the beast, J.D. bent to inspect each of its pancake-size hooves in turn. "Don't worry," he said without straightening. "This old boy is nice and gentle, and he moves like a rocking chair."

"Now who's stretching the truth?" she muttered.

J.D. glanced up. "Not me, city girl."

"I wasn't raised in New York, you know. Boise is hardly the center of modern civilization."

"Compared to the ranch or the rez, it is." He straightened. "Duke's rarin' to go."

"But he's so big," she protested, eyeing the distance from Duke's back to the hard floor. "Don't you have something built a little closer to the ground?"

"You mean like a sports car?" he asked. "Or did you expect to start out on Rose's pony?"

Kirby had to smile at the image his words conjured up—of herself perched on a Shetland pony with her legs dangling almost to the ground. "Could I?" she asked, only half kidding. "That way I wouldn't have so far to fall."

His gaze sharpened. "What makes you think I'd let you fall?"

The absolute seriousness of his question startled her and she glanced away. "I don't know."

He waited until she looked back at him. To her surprise, his expression had softened. "You'll be safe with me."

Recalling his brusque understanding on the night she'd stumbled upon his house, Kirby realized that she believed him utterly and that most of her jitters were gone, replaced by a tiny bud of anticipation. If this was how he gentled horses, no wonder her brother thought J.D. was the best trainer in the state.

"Like I told you, it's been a long time," she mumbled as he watched her steadily.

"Easy as falling off a log," he began, and then shook his head. "Or should I say, easy as riding a bicycle?"

It had taken her months to learn how to balance on a two-wheeler. "That's not as encouraging as you might think."

"You'll be fine." He disappeared into the tack

room, momentarily releasing her from the spell of his gaze.

Cautiously, Kirby extended a hand to Duke, who huffed out a warm breath that tickled her fingers. Encouraged, she rubbed his soft nose, never taking her eyes from his big yellow teeth.

"Good boy."

J.D. returned, wearing an amused expression and lugging a huge saddle. "I'll tack him up, but after this you're on your own. A good rider knows how to take care of her mount." He spent a few minutes demonstrating what to do. When he had tightened the cinch, he straightened and thrust the reins into her hands. "He's all yours."

Kirby stared at them, then back at J.D., who was headed for the arena. "What do I do with these?" she asked.

"Hang on to them and follow me."

Kirby glanced behind her. "What about Duke?"

J.D.'s laughter floated back to her, as warm as the sunshine streaming in the high windows. "Don't worry about him. He'll come with you as long as you don't let go of the reins. If you drop them, though, he won't budge. He's trained to stay put when he's ground-tied."

Kirby knew what that meant from watching old westerns on television. Cautiously, she led Duke into the arena where J.D. was checking the rigging on his buckskin.

"Can you mount by yourself?" he asked. "Once you're in the saddle, we'll adjust the stirrups."

She wasn't about to admit that she had no idea whether she could get on Duke without a ladder. Gripping the horn with both hands, she slipped her boot into the stirrup. As her other foot left the ground, Duke sidestepped and she let out a little squeak of dismay. Before she could blink, J.D. was behind her.

"Don't panic, I've got you," he said, clamping his hands around her waist. "Try it now."

His firm grip was distracting. How was she supposed to hike herself up when her bones had just been turned to water?

His hands tightened. "Ready?" he asked.

Breathless, she managed to nod. He was standing so close that she could feel the heat of his body and breathe in his scent, a combination of after-shave, leather and horse.

J.D. was so busy studying all the different shades of hair woven into her braid, from the dark, rich color of fireweed honey all the way to the pale gold of a full desert moon, that he nearly missed the faint bob of her head. Then he noticed the wink of gold at her ear and saw that it was a tiny starfish. Below it, the skin of her nape was so finely grained that it appeared poreless. He'd actually lifted his hand to brush aside the strands of hair that had worked loose from her braid when he caught himself.

Returning his grip to her waist, he heard her smothered gasp as he lifted her. Then she was scrambling into place in the saddle as he stepped away.

As she looked around from her lofty perch, Kirby told herself the increase in her heart rate was only because the air had to be thinner so far off the ground.

"Okay?" J.D. asked, clearly unaffected by her nearness.

"Okay," she echoed.

"Try to relax." He patted her calf absently before walking to his own horse. While Kirby watched, he swung his leg awkwardly across Buck's back. Once he was seated, though, he underwent a startling transformation.

Kirby's breath snagged in her chest at the sight of him poised there as naturally as if he and the horse had somehow melded into one entity, not unlike the centaurs of ancient mythology. Even J.D.'s expression shed its tenseness, his eyes squeezed shut as if he were savoring a moment of perfect harmony.

The tiny lapse made her aware of just how often his physical limitations must chafe at him. What had he thought the other night when she'd carried on so over the long-ago demise of parents she couldn't remember, when he knew real loss—a career snatched away from him because he'd put the safety of a child ahead of his own dreams? The realization humbled her and made her determined to be more tolerant of his apparent aloofness.

Sending him a brilliant smile that had him eyeing her suspiciously, she waited patiently for him to start her lesson. Tugging down the brim of his Stetson, he began rapping out a series of brief commands that Kirby followed the best she could. When she didn't understand exactly what he wanted, he demonstrated.

Following his instructions, she urged Duke into a walk, turning him first one way and then the other in the small arena. J.D. observed her as closely as if she'd been auditioning for the Olympic equestrian team, and occasionally made a suggestion. By the time he finally called a halt, she'd gotten over the sensation of being too far off the ground and was actually enjoying herself.

"We'd better stop for today or you'll be too sore

to ride tomorrow. Your muscles aren't used to this kind of workout.''

"I feel fine." Kirby glanced down at her watch, surprised at how much time had gone by. She'd expected him to race through the lesson as quickly as possible.

"If your legs bother you later, take a warm bath," he suggested, dismounting with relative ease.

"Thanks for your time," she said, unable to resist adding, "I hope I wasn't too much of a greenhorn for you."

His eyes narrowed briefly, emphasizing the tiny lines etched at their outer corners, but he didn't comment. Instead, he held up his arms to her.

"You may need help getting down," he explained when she merely stared at his outstretched hand.

"I can manage." Freeing one foot from the stirrup, Kirby swung her leg over Duke's broad back the same way she'd seen J.D. do. She was about to lower herself to the ground when the muscles of her thigh gave out abruptly. Simultaneously, her grip slipped off the saddle horn.

She'd started tumbling backward into a graceless heap when J.D. snagged her in his arms. Crashing against him, she drove the air from his chest in a muffled *whoof* as he staggered to regain his balance. His arms tightened around her like steel bands.

"I'm sorry," she gasped, humiliated, as he made sure she was solid on her feet.

"It's my fault," he contradicted. "I let you ride too long for the first time." His voice was husky as he released her. When she turned to argue, he was standing so close that she could see the dark whiskers on his upper lip and around his mouth. Her mind emptied, leaving her dizzy, and she stared mutely.

His head dipped toward hers as the air around them crackled with electricity, then his brows jerked upward and he backed away so fast that he stumbled. Automatically, Kirby caught at his forearm to steady him.

Dusky color flooded his cheeks. Roughly, he shrugged off her hand. Heart pounding with embarrassment, she folded her arms across her chest and stared at the ground. The incident had happened so fast—she was only sure it had happened at all by the tingling of her lips where his gaze had seared them.

"I'm sorry," she said again, painfully aware of his humiliation as well as her own. As if she cared that he might not always be surefooted. Then she realized how much it must matter to him. Senses humming, she dared to look up, into eyes that were as opaque as black paint in a face devoid of expression.

"Wear warm clothes tomorrow," was all he said. "You're ready to go outside."

"Are you sure?" she asked, surprised he didn't relegate her instead to the pony ring.

J.D. set his hands on his hips and tipped back his head. "Are you questioning my judgment, city girl?" he asked with cool arrogance.

Just as coolly, she replied, "I wouldn't dream of it, cowboy."

He narrowed his eyes, but she thought she saw his lips twitch.

"What shall I do with my horse?" she asked as Duke blew out a long breath.

"I'll deal with him this time," J.D. replied, taking the reins from her unresisting fingers.

She hesitated, hoping he might comment on her performance, but he merely instructed her to be there at the same time the next day before he led the animals away.

Realizing that she was staring after him like a groupie watching a rock star, Kirby wheeled around and headed for the door. Only then, as her legs trembled beneath her in silent protest, did she understand what he'd meant. Walking carefully, she vowed that she'd be there for the next day's lesson if she had to soak in a hot bath all night.

J.D. watched her walk away on long legs that appeared slightly shaky. He felt guilty for having kept her in the saddle for so long, but he'd been torn between the need to escape and the greedy desire to be close to her. A bad sign. Usually he had no trouble ignoring temptation, but this woman was different, and that very difference drew him like a coyote to a baited trap.

He'd have to be careful, he told himself, or he'd end up with the same fate as the coyote.

"Honey, we all want you to stay, not just Donovan," Bobbie told Kirby over a dinner of potatoes and frozen peas from their own garden, chicken with creamy gravy and light-as-air dumplings made from scratch. "A couple of weeks isn't enough time to really get to know each other again."

Blinking back tears, Kirby glanced at Rose, who was watching the adults while she toyed with her vegetables.

"Please stay, Aunt Kirby," she said, brown eyes round with anxiety. "We don't want you to go."

"Thank you, honey." Turning to Donovan, Kirby demanded, "Have you been coaching this child?"

Wearing a patently innocent expression, he shook his head. "I didn't have to. She's not saying anything her mom and I don't want, as well."

"I'm not sure how to respond." Kirby thought of the parents she'd left behind in Idaho—and whom she had yet to forgive for their deceit—as well as her friends and her job at the clinic. She missed Jill and couldn't expect the doctor's wife to fill in for her indefinitely. Kirby might lose the position if she stayed here any longer.

"Why not think about making Colorado your permanent home?" Donovan reached across the table to cover her hand with his larger one. "We've got plenty of room for you here."

"I hadn't considered staying on," Kirby said honestly. Her friends were back in Boise; then again, so was Tim, her ex-husband. Never seeing *him* again would be no hardship, not after the painful way their marriage had ended.

She was about to add that she couldn't make up her mind about such an important issue right away when the phone rang, interrupting her. With an apologetic glance, Donovan rose to answer it.

"It's for you," he told her after he had listened for a moment. "If you'd like, you can take it in my office."

Who would be calling her here? Kirby wondered as she thanked him and hurried down the hall to the phone on his desk.

"Sis, this is Jon. How are you?"

Her adopted brother's familiar voice sent a warm feeling through her. She'd talked to him only once since Donovan first appeared, and Jonnie had been as shocked as she was to find out she'd been adopted. Six years her junior, Jonathan Gaard Wilson was his parents' natural son. He and his former college art-history professor had opened an exclusive furniture gallery in Aspen, but he'd kept in touch with Kirby despite the distance separating them. Family ties were precious to both of them and she knew Jon's loyalties were strained by her break with their parents.

"I've been having a great time," she told him now. "I'm even learning to ride horses. In fact, Donovan and I were just discussing the possibility of extending my visit."

There was a brief silence at the other end of the line. "What about your job?" Jon asked. "I thought you enjoyed your work at the clinic."

"I do, but I could probably find something here," she replied. "I haven't had much chance to think about it yet."

"If you do stay on, perhaps we could get together," he suggested. "I'd like you to meet Martin and see what we've done with the store."

After Kirby had agreed enthusiastically, Jon cleared his throat. "Have you spoken to the folks?" he asked.

"No. Have you?" She didn't want to put him on the spot, but she wondered what he might have heard. Were the Wilsons sorry for deceiving her or did they still insist they'd done it for her own good?

"Mom's called a couple of times. They both miss you a lot."

Kirby didn't bother to reply. She was still angry. "Are they well?" she asked instead.

"They seem to be."

"Thanks for not lecturing me," she felt compelled

to say. Growing up, she'd sometimes lectured him. Since he and Martin had moved to Aspen, Kirby had remained one of Jon's staunchest supporters.

"I don't have the right to lecture anyone, but it would be nice if you called them up, just to tell them you're okay," he suggested.

"I'm not ready."

"I understand. Then would you mind if I told them that I'd talked to you?" he asked.

"That would be all right, I guess." She gripped the receiver a little tighter. Perhaps she was being unreasonable to feel such resentment toward the couple who had raised her as their own, but she needed time to work out her feelings.

As her gaze fell on the little horse J.D. had carved, she realized with sudden insight that she wasn't ready to go back to Boise. Not yet. "When you call, tell them I'm staying here for a while. I'll get Jill to pack up the rest of my things." Kirby's decision, though impulsive, felt right once she had voiced it aloud.

After she'd asked after Martin and the gallery, there was another pause before she heard Jon sigh. Silently, Kirby braced herself.

"The folks love you, and I'm sure they were only doing what they thought was best. Just think about talking to them, okay?"

"I'll think about it," she promised. "And I'll call you back after I know more about my plans."

When she had told him goodbye and returned to the dining room, the three Buchanans looked up at her expectantly.

"That was my adopted brother, Jonathan," she explained as Bobbie began serving dessert, a peach cobbler with ice cream. "He has a business in Aspen."

"We'll have to invite him down for dinner," Bobbie said. "I'd love to meet him."

Kirby gave her a grateful smile, but had something more pressing on her mind. "If the offer's still open, I'd like to stay," she told Donovan.

A grin spread across his handsome face as he jumped to his feet and enveloped her in a fierce bear hug. "That's great, sis." His voice was muffled against her hair, but she could hear the emotion he made no attempt to hide. The sincerity of his feelings for her was a continuing source of delight, and she felt incredibly lucky that he'd tried so hard to find her.

When he finally let her go, Bobbie and Rose were waiting to hug her as well.

"Now we can go riding together all over the country," Rose told her as they all sat back down.

"After I've had a couple more lessons," Kirby replied. "J.D. said I'm ready to go outside tomorrow, though."

"I meant to ask how it went," Donovan told her around a spoonful of peach cobbler. "How did you get along with Reese?"

"Fine." After a soak in the tub, her legs weren't even that sore. Now she told herself that J.D. had nothing to do with her decision to stick around. It wasn't as if she had anything in common with the former bull rider, even if he was one of the most intriguing men she'd ever met. No doubt he'd only prevented his dog from chewing her up the other night to save himself the trouble of explaining her sudden disappearance to his boss. "Mr. Reese is a patient teacher."

Donovan's eyebrows lifted, and then he nodded. "I

shouldn't be surprised. He took time with Rose, helped her over her fear. Now she loves to ride, don't you, babe?''

"J.D.'s the best," she agreed, "next to my daddy."

Donovan winked at her, then turned back to Kirby. "You've got a home with us as long as you want."

"But I can't freeload off you indefinitely," she cautioned him. "If I'm going to stay on, I need to find some kind of temporary job."

"That's not necessary," he exclaimed.

"It is to me. I can't let you support me," she argued. "I'm a nurse. I need to work."

"How can we get to know each other if you're working all the time?" Donovan demanded, frowning.

"I won't be gone twenty-four hours a day."

"Still—" he began.

"Still," she echoed playfully, "I may not even be able to find anything full-time."

The frown creasing his forehead melted away. "You don't have to work at all, you know. There's enough to keep you busy around here if you're afraid you'd get bored. You could even be the ranch medical consultant."

"And do what?" she asked. "Hand out aspirin to the men and remove their slivers?"

"Someone has to do it." Donovan's voice held an underlying hint of persistence. He hadn't gotten as far as he had by accepting defeat easily, Kirby realized, but she could dig in her heels, too. Eventually, he'd come around. She saw how he indulged both Bobbie and Rose. He'd fall in line when he realized how much it meant to Kirby to feel she was contributing something toward her upkeep.

"I'll have to find out if Colorado has a reciprocal agreement with Idaho, so I can get licensed to work here," she murmured. "I'll have to make some calls tomorrow."

"There's no hurry." Donovan sipped his coffee.

"Now, sweetheart, let her do what she needs to," Bobbie coaxed. "You got what you wanted. She's agreed to stay."

The unexpected support pleased Kirby, who gave her sister-in-law a grateful smile.

"I'll tell Reese to plan on more riding lessons," Donovan said over the rim of his cup. "Before you know it, you'll be sitting a horse like a regular Annie Oakley."

She ought to feel guilty for taking up more of J.D.'s time, Kirby thought, but it wasn't guilt she felt when she pictured herself racing across the plains on horseback with him hot on her heels—it was a mixture of breathless anticipation and pure fear.

Chapter Five

When Kirby reported to the stable for her next riding lesson, Rose went with her. Despite Kirby's misgivings about making a fool of herself in front of a five-year-old, she welcomed her niece's company as a buffer between herself and the cowboy she suspected would rather clean stalls than spend time with her.

"Hi, Petunia." When she and Rose walked into the stables, J.D. came out of the stall where he'd been brushing a black horse with spots on its rump. He was wearing a red plaid shirt and dark jeans.

Rose's giggles were so infectious that Kirby smiled at him despite the mere nod of acknowledgment he gave her. She watched the stark lines of his face relax, making him even more attractive as he listened attentively to Rose's latest lecture about remembering her name.

"It's like the ranch," she concluded earnestly, tiny hands curled into fists on her denim-covered hips. "The Rocking Rose."

Beneath the brim of his hat, J.D.'s brows shot up. "Your name is Rocking Rose?" he asked with mock seriousness. "All this time I thought it was Rose Buchanan."

"See?" she exclaimed, pointing an accusing finger. "You do remember."

"I guess you caught me." He glanced again at Kirby, the remainder of his smile still gleaming in his dark eyes. "Ready for another lesson?" he asked.

Her anxiety over riding outside began to fade. "I guess so."

In a few minutes, she found herself once again in the saddle, staring at J.D.'s back as he led the way down a dirt road she'd been on before in Donovan's Jeep. A line of fence was the only thing that broke the flat expanse of brownish grass, a lone bird overhead the only other living creature in sight.

Kirby turned and waved at Rose, who was riding Peanut Butter, her Palomino pony. Drumming his chubby sides with the heels of her red boots, she urged him along. "This is fun," Rose exclaimed.

The day was a mild one, with the fall sun shining brightly and the breeze just strong enough to cool Kirby's heated cheeks. While she inhaled the clean air with lazy contentment and listened to the jangle of bridles and the creak of saddle leather, J.D. slowed Buck until he was riding alongside her.

"We're going to speed things up a little," he said as Duke extended an inquisitive muzzle toward the other gelding. "Don't worry. Just feel for the rhythm of your horse and let your body go with it."

"Sounds simple enough," she muttered as panic began creeping in.

"Ready?"

"As I'll ever be."

With quiet command, he sent his mount leaping forward, and Kirby gritted her teeth as Duke did the same. At first she expected to be bounced from the saddle and crushed beneath Peanut Butter's diminutive hooves. Then, as Duke's jarring trot smoothed into a flowing canter and her body began adjusting to the movements, she understood what J.D. had meant.

"You're doing good, Aunt Kirby!" Rose called from behind her.

J.D. was riding slightly ahead and to the side, checking her progress over his shoulder. When she caught his gaze, he nodded his approval. Surprised, Kirby realized she was enjoying the sensation of flying along the ground.

All too soon, J.D. reined in his horse. With a sigh of disappointment, Kirby slowed Duke to a walk as Rose, whose pony's short legs had failed to keep pace, caught up with them.

"She's borned on the saddle, just like me, isn't she?" Rose demanded of J.D. Her words made Kirby's flush of pleasure deepen. Still, she found herself searching his face eagerly for some sign that he agreed.

"Born to the saddle," J.D. corrected gently. "She's not nearly as good as you, honey," he drawled, "but she shows definite promise."

Absurdly pleased, Kirby flashed a smile that encompassed both him and her niece. "Pretty soon I'll be racing you," she promised Rose rashly. "We can ride all over the ranch together."

"I thought you were going home in just a few days." J.D.'s relaxed expression had sharpened imperceptibly.

"I've extended my visit," she replied, watching carefully for any sign that her change of plans mattered to him one way or the other. "I may just make this ranch my permanent home."

"Isn't that great?" Rose asked, oblivious of the undercurrents flowing around her. "Aunt Kirby might live with us *forever*."

J.D. kept his face devoid of expression, but his gut was churning with a jumble of mixed reactions. A surge of fierce pleasure whipped through him, and then he reminded himself that her decision to stay had nothing to do with *him*.

"Great," he echoed flatly, his gaze fixed on Kirby. Apparently she was in no hurry to abandon a cushy situation with her successful brother in order to return to whatever she'd left in Idaho.

"Don't you have anyone waiting for you back home?" he demanded, not sure why he found her news so unnerving. "I meant friends or family," he added hastily, not wanting her to assume he was asking about a boyfriend. *He* certainly didn't care if she had a half-dozen potato farmers after her.

Briefly, a shadow crossed her face. Then she tossed her head. "No one important," she said, making him wonder who'd captured her thoughts for that fleeting moment. Had someone hurt her? "The family that matters to me is here, and I can make new friends."

J.D. glanced at Rose, who was watching the two of them with a perplexed expression on her round face. "It's time to go back," he said, reining Buck around so abruptly that the horse half reared in protest. "I've got a heavy schedule today and the vet's coming out."

He saw Rose and Kirby exchange glances, and he wondered if his annoyance showed. All he knew was that Kirby's unexpected announcement had triggered a rash of feelings. Normally he wasn't a deeply analytical man, but it worried him that he had no clue to what any of them meant.

"I got a job!" Kirby announced as she burst into the kitchen, where Bobbie was stirring a steaming kettle on the six-burner stove. Donovan stood close to her with one arm hooked around her waist and his bare head bent as if he'd been whispering something for her ears alone.

"Oops. I'll, uh, catch you later."

Sorry to have interrupted what must have been a rare moment of privacy while Rose was away at afternoon kindergarten, Kirby started backing out of the kitchen. The delicious aroma of homemade soup followed her, making her stomach rumble hollowly and reminding her that she hadn't eaten since early that morning.

"That's great, hon." Before she could make good her escape, Bobbie gave her a friendly smile and a thumbs-up.

"Way to go, sis. Don't run off." Letting his arm fall to his side, Donovan pulled out a kitchen chair and straddled it, fastening the first three snaps of his shirt without any apparent embarrassment. He was dressed in the same uniform the ranch hands wore—a plaid wool shirt and jeans with a wide leather belt and battered boots. "Did you fill that opening at the

Miller Clinic?'' He plucked an apple from the bowl on the table and took a large bite.

Bobbie's cheeks were rosy, more so than slaving over a hot stove warranted. With a sudden ache, Kirby envied them their obvious affection for each other.

"Actually, I didn't take that job." She sat down across from him.

In the few days since she had decided to stay on in Colorado, she had dealt with the necessary paperwork so she could practice her nursing skills here and had registered at several agencies. Just this morning she'd had two interviews, one of them at a clinic run by a friend of her brothers.

Now she braced herself for Donovan's disappointment. The Miller Medical Clinic was a modern facility, the doctor progressive and pleasant, but as she'd listened to him describing her duties, she realized she needed something more. A real challenge.

Donovan looked surprised. "Didn't you like Dave Miller?" he asked as he wiped his mouth. Then a sudden frown marred his attractive features. "Or didn't he offer you the job?" Setting down the apple, he unfolded his tall frame from the kitchen chair and patted her shoulder. "I'll call him and get this sorted out. He owes me a couple of favors."

His reaction wasn't what Kirby had expected, but she should have gotten used to his take-charge attitude by now. Panic-stricken, she glanced at Bobbie, who was watching the two of them with an amused expression.

"You don't understand," Kirby told her brother, heading him off before he could reach the phone. "I didn't want to work at the clinic."

"Why not?" he demanded. "You said you landed a job, even though I told you it wasn't necessary."

"It's necessary to me." She had to remind herself that Donovan didn't know her very well yet, didn't understand her need for independence.

"Didn't he offer you enough money?" he persisted.

"The figure he quoted was adequate, but money wasn't the main issue."

Now her brother really appeared confused. "Then what was?"

Renewed excitement bubbled up inside her, validating the choice she'd made. "The job at the clinic was perfect," she explained. "Almost identical to the one I had in Boise."

Donovan threw up his hands in a gesture of sheer male exasperation. "I don't understand."

Patiently, Kirby said, "I've decided to work as a visiting nurse instead. It will probably be for only a couple of days a week, at least at first, but the duties are so much more varied than weighing patients and taking their temperatures. I want the responsibility and the challenge. I hope you're not too disappointed."

"You mean you'll be making house calls?" Donovan asked with an incredulous expression. "On your own?"

"Of course. That's what a visiting nurse does. I'll treat people who can't get in to see a doctor because they're too old or too poor, mostly, and they live too far from town. They need someone to come out and change a dressing, take out stitches, things like that."

"You'll be doing a lot of driving?"

"Yes, but I'd need my own transportation, anyway.

Can you suggest someplace I can buy a used car? The one I had back in Idaho isn't in good-enough shape to bring out. I was going to trade it in pretty soon anyway, so I'll just have a friend sell it for me. I'm sure Jill wouldn't mind.'' Kirby didn't want Donovan to think she expected him to buy her a car, although, knowing his generous nature, he probably would if she needed him to. "I'm not picky as long as it's reliable,'' she added. Winter in Boise could be fierce; no doubt rural Colorado was even worse.

Rubbing his fingers along his jaw, Donovan appeared to be considering her request. "You don't know your way around this country,'' he said after a moment. "How are you going to find these patients you're planning to visit?''

"Now, honey,'' Bobbie interrupted, "I'm sure she's thought about all this.''

Kirby took a moment to remind herself that he was no doubt playing devil's advocate. Looking out for a younger sister, even when they were both adults, was probably a novelty, and he just needed time to adjust. "I'll learn my way around,'' she said brightly. "I bought a map.''

"A lot of the places you'll be going aren't on any map,'' he argued. "Some of them probably don't even have real addresses.''

She'd been given a vague description of the territory she'd be covering, but she'd been too excited about the work itself to pay much attention.

"I'll manage,'' she replied confidently, "but I will need to buy a car before I start. Maybe a station wagon or a pickup truck would be a good idea.'' She liked the image of herself driving a big half-ton.

"What you need is a four-by-four,'' he countered.

"I don't want you getting stuck in a snowdrift in some godforsaken corner of the county, waiting for help that may take its sweet time coming." A visible shudder went through him, and Kirby wondered if he was thinking of their parents' accident. "You have no idea how quickly the weather can change here," he added earnestly. "A blizzard can catch you unexpectedly. An icy road can send you into a ditch. Can't you wait until next spring to take this job?"

"It might not be available next spring," she replied. The director had told her they always needed good nurses, but she had no intention of sharing that bit of information with her overprotective brother— or of sitting on her hands all winter. She needed to be earning money of her own.

For a moment, Donovan chewed on his lower lip. "You'll just have to call and tell them you've changed your mind," he said imperiously. "This whole idea is crazy."

Bobbie had been tasting the contents of the soup pot. At his pronouncement, the spoon froze in her hand. "Honey—" she began.

Kirby had no wish for the two of them to argue over her. Besides, she could fight her own battles. "Why on earth would I tell them that?" she interrupted, finally beginning to run out of patience with his attitude. "I took this job because it sounds exciting and different. It's exactly what I was looking for."

Donovan started shaking his head before she even finished talking. "You don't understand. I just can't let you take the risk. It would be too dangerous."

Bobbie had set down the spoon and was watching them with a worried expression.

"Let me?" Kirby echoed. She turned to Bobbie, incensed. "Is he always this dictatorial?"

"Not usually, but he has his moments." Her tone was dry.

Donovan swiveled his head. "Sweetheart, you know I'm right. She has no idea what she could be facing out there alone."

Bobbie just groaned and threw up her hands. "I'm not saying that you don't have a good point, just that your presentation is flawed."

The muscles in his jaw bunched, giving him a mutinous expression. "I don't see why."

"She's not Rose," Bobbie reminded him.

His frown deepened. "I know that."

"Perhaps you'd just like to marry me off to some neighbor whose land joins yours," Kirby sputtered.

"Huh?" His face mirrored his obvious confusion. "Why would I do that? I just don't want you going off the road somewhere, alone and lost, that's all." His words confirmed Kirby's suspicion that their parents' accident was lurking in the back of his mind.

Bobbie crossed the kitchen to plant her hand on his shoulder. "I understand your concerns, love, but I think you could have worded them a little more tactfully." Tenderly, she touched his cheek. "How about a compromise? What if someone went along with her for a while, just until she learns her way around?"

"That's a good—" Donovan stopped abruptly as Kirby got to her feet. "Where are you going?"

"To pack," she said grimly. She didn't need a chaperon or a guide. "If I can't work, I can't stay."

"I never said you couldn't work," he replied.

"You want to assign me a baby-sitter."

"Not a baby-sitter," Donovan argued. "Someone

to drive you temporarily, a ranch hand I'd be paying to sit on his behind while the work's slow or one I'd have to lay off for the winter, otherwise. Look at it as saving a man's job as well as your brother's peace of mind,'' he wheedled shamelessly. ''I'd feel better if you'd do this, at least until the weather's better. It would keep me from going prematurely gray.''

''Oh, please.'' Studying him, Kirby glimpsed the loving concern behind the iron-jawed determination. She began to relent by slow degrees. How could she begrudge Donovan his chance to play big brother after he'd searched for her for so long?

She sighed, about to give in, and then another thought assailed her. ''Just who would you get to go with me?''

He shrugged. ''How about Charlie Babcock? He's young, but he's as strong as a bull, and he's a likable-enough guy. If you were to get stuck in a drift, Charlie could wrestle you out.''

''That's a good idea,'' Bobbie murmured, looking anxiously at Kirby. ''Don't you think so?''

Before she could reply, a knock sounded at the back door. Looking up, Kirby glimpsed J.D. through the glass.

''Sorry to interrupt,'' he said, sweeping his hat from his head when Bobbie had let him in, ''but the vet wants to see you. Pretty Boy's down. It looks like colic.'' There was a dusting of new snow on the shoulders of his quilted vest and his cheeks were red from the cold. His unexpected appearance made Kirby's heart thud hard as his gaze touched hers briefly.

As J.D. turned down Bobbie's offer of coffee, Donovan got to his feet. ''I'm sorry,'' he told Kirby as she scrambled to remember what on earth they'd been discussing. "I'd better go. Can we talk later?"

"Of course." Charlie Babcock had seemed pleasant enough when she'd met him, even though he'd blushed to the roots of his hair. She sneaked a look at J.D. Apparently, her taste ran to the more exotic male. Still, she wasn't convinced that she needed an escort. "I hope Pretty Boy's okay," she added. She remembered that J.D. had said he was a promising colt and that they had high hopes for him in the show ring.

Donovan's expression cleared. "So do I. Thanks, sis." Bending to give Bobbie a quick kiss, he grabbed his hat and jacket from a hook by the door and followed J.D. outside.

"He's certainly attractive, isn't he?" Bobbie murmured after the two men had left.

"Of course," Kirby replied proudly. "He's my brother."

Bobbie's grin widened. "Not Donovan," she corrected, "although I do think he's the handsomest man in Colorado. I was referring to J.D."

It was Kirby's turn to blush. "If you like the type." She studied her folded hands.

Bobbie chuckled as she pulled out a chair and sat down. "Don't try to convince me that you're immune," she teased. "I've seen the way you look at him. And the way he tries not to look back at you."

Kirby gaped at the other woman. Had she been that obvious? Worse yet, had J.D. caught her mooning over him? Oh, Lord, say it wasn't so! Was that why he did his best to ignore her existence? "He doesn't even like me," she blurted.

Elbows on the table, Bobbie propped her chin on

her linked hands. "This gets better and better," she mused. "Why do you think that?"

"You're as bad as my brother!' Kirby exclaimed, getting to her feet. "Matchmaking might run in the family, but I think you should direct your efforts to someone who needs them. I don't happen to be in the market for a man right now."

"Why not?" Bobbie asked, clearly unrepentant. "Don't you find him intriguing? A little dangerous?"

Kirby hesitated. "Maybe," she admitted cautiously, "but the last thing I need is a fling with a cowboy."

Now Bobbie's grin widened shamelessly. "Take it from me, hon," she urged. "A fling with a cowboy can do wonders. Maybe it's J.D. who should drive you around instead of Charlie."

As J.D. left the stable where he'd been cleaning tack, he saw Kirby waiting by her silver Bronco. She was bareheaded, her hair shining in the light from a pale sun that did little to lessen the chill in the late fall air. Snow had been forecast, but so far there hadn't been a flake in sight.

Kirby didn't look like any nurse he'd ever seen, her cheeks wind-washed above the collar of her bulky red parka. With it she wore jeans and practical black boots. Boots that probably cost more than he made in a month.

At the sight of her, J.D. was disconcerted to feel the sharp tug of attraction he should have under control by now. As he continued to watch her hungrily, she spotted him and the smile on her full mouth faltered.

She must have been put off by the way he was

dressed, but the horses didn't care what he wore and he'd had no idea he'd be recruited to fill in for Charlie. The young cowhand had been rushed to the hospital with appendicitis late last night. Now J.D., who'd been dragged from the stall he'd been cleaning and pressed into service moments before by his boss, was acutely conscious of his own rundown boots, their scars and worn spots partially covered by frayed jeans he'd climbed into before first light this morning. With them he'd pulled on a patched flannel shirt and a lined denim jacket that could have been cleaner.

Since Big Mike, plagued by arthritis, had abruptly decided to retire to his daughter's home in Florida, and the other cowhands were busy delivering feed to the cattle, there was no one left to chauffeur Kirby in her new job except J.D. At least that was what Buchanan had told him. J.D. had been tempted to suggest Donovan go with her himself.

What was the point in her working if she couldn't handle the job on her own? he wondered. Not that he liked the idea of her out there by herself dealing with some of the characters he'd met since he'd come here. Why couldn't she work in a hospital, where she'd be safe and could stay out of his way at the same time?

"I appreciate your filling in like this," Buchanan told him quietly before they got to the Bronco, where Kirby waited. "It should only be for a few days, but let me know if you need more help in the stable and we'll figure out something."

Great. One more reason for the man to feel indebted. "Yeah, whatever," J.D. muttered, figuring it was his woodcarving that would suffer, not the horses. "Driving around a good-looking blonde beats cleaning stalls any day of the week."

Buchanan hesitated, as J.D. had meant him to. Even shorthanded as they were, there had to be someone else who could play nursemaid. Someone who didn't wake up in a sweat at night after dreams that involved him, her and things a gentleman didn't mention, even when he couldn't stop thinking about them. J.D. tried hard not to think about sharing the intimacy of that vehicle with her. Tried not to think about keeping his hands wrapped around the steering wheel until he could no longer fight the temptation to pull over and bury his face in her hair, pressing his mouth against the lushness of hers. Imagining it made him shake.

He was tempted to head for the barn, but he knew, deep down, that there was no one else he'd trust to look out for her the way he could. Let anyone try to bother her while she was with him and he'd take him apart. It would be one way to work off some of his frustration.

Jaw locked with determination, he headed for the Bronco. And hoped he wasn't walking into disaster.

"I could have changed that tire myself." Kirby said as J.D. slowed for a turn. She pictured the way he'd looked, hunkered down by the wheel as he made the switch with easy efficiency while clouds gathered above them. Deep down, she knew it would have taken her twice as long to wrestle the wheel free—if she could've gotten the bolts loose in the first place.

Without taking his gaze from the dirt road that stretched before them like a rutted brown ribbon, J.D. told her, "That's what I'm here for, making sure you don't break a nail or get lost in the wilderness."

Irritated, Kirby held up her hands. "My nails are fine, thanks anyway. And I haven't gotten lost yet."

"Then I must be doing my job, right?"

She didn't bother to answer. In the last couple of weeks, she'd learned to ignore his more outrageous comments instead of jumping to refute them, just as she'd learned, at least partly, to ignore the attraction that simmered through her blood like the fizz from champagne whenever she was around him.

Until now their uneasy partnership had gone relatively smoothly, she thought with a wry grimace. She had made suggestions and he'd ignored them. She had tried to initiate conversations and he'd refused to reply. She had hoped the response she felt to his presence beside her in the Bronco would die a natural death and, so far, it had tenaciously refused.

"Save your strength for counting out pills and unrolling bandages." His tone was mocking, but the corner of his mouth twitched. She suspected he enjoyed teasing her. Or he just liked getting away from the stable occasionally.

When the word had come back from the hospital that Charlie's appendix had ruptured and he would be recuperating for several weeks, J.D. had apparently resigned himself to driving her whenever the weather was especially bad or her destination was difficult to find. More than once when she was alone, she'd been forced to call the office on the cellular phone she always carried and ask for more detailed directions.

Once she'd gotten lost, and a hunter had led her back to the main road. He'd told her he had a daughter about her age. Despite the difficulties, Kirby enjoyed the work and the people she met.

Just yesterday she'd locked horns with a stubborn old Ute who refused to let her clean up a cut on his leg that had gotten infected. Only after J.D. had interceded, trading on his own part-Navajo heritage, did the man reluctantly allow her to treat him. She'd been tempted to ask J.D. more about his background, but had managed to hold her tongue. The week before he'd helped her lift a big woman with a sprained ankle into the wheelchair they delivered, and once he'd persuaded a little girl to be vaccinated by letting Kirby stick a needle in his own arm first.

Now they were on their way out to recheck a woman whose third child was due in less than a month. She had no transportation except a battered, rusty car of ancient vintage and dubious reliability, so Kirby had persuaded a neighbor to drive her to the hospital when her time came. Prenatal checkups, though, weren't high on the neighbor's priority list.

"I'll just be a few minutes," she told J.D. when they pulled up in front of a small, one-story house. There was no telephone, but a television antenna was attached to the patched roof. The bathroom was out back.

Sliding from the passenger seat, Kirby grabbed her medical bag. As usual, J.D. didn't reply. He got out from behind the wheel and leaned against the fender with a pocketknife and a small piece of wood.

When Kirby knocked on the peeling front door, it was opened by a little boy with dark eyes and straight black hair.

When he stared mutely, Kirby introduced herself. "Where's your mom?" she asked gently.

The child's lower lip began to tremble and tears filled his eyes, but all he did was jam one thumb into his mouth.

A premonition rippled through Kirby and she

glanced back at J.D., who immediately straightened from his post against the Bronco.

"Trouble?" he asked.

"I'm not sure." Even before she heard Anna Szabo's groan of pain, though, Kirby expected a problem.

Giving the boy what she hoped was a confident smile, she hurried to the bedroom, where it took her only a moment to assess the situation. Kirby offered the expectant mother a few comforting words, distracted the boy and his younger sister with picture books from her bag and did a quick exam. Then she went back to the door to call J.D. As an obstetrics assistant, he might not be much, but he was all she had and the woman was fully dilated.

J.D. was whittling the wood into a shape that reminded Kirby of the small bird she kept on the nightstand next to her bed. His head was bent, long hair screening his expression, and his rangy shoulders were slightly hunched against the wind.

"Would you come in here, please?" she called to him. "I need your help."

His black brows rose in question as he straightened, closing his pocketknife and tucking it and the carving into his shirt pocket. "What is it?" he asked, limp barely discernible as he came over to where she waited.

"This baby is on its way," she said. "There's no time to get Anna to a hospital."

The unreadable expression on his face barely flickered. "What do you want me to do?"

At least he hadn't panicked at the news. Not yet. "Take the kids to the neighbor's. Then come back and help me."

He frowned. "Help you with what?"

She took a deep breath. "It looks as if you and I are going to deliver this baby."

Chapter Six

"I can see the baby's head. You're doing a great job." Although perspiration beaded Kirby's forehead and her moss green eyes were shadowed with the fatigue of a long day, her voice remained steady and encouraging as the other woman strained to give birth to her child. "One last push, Anna, that's the way."

It had been a little over half an hour since Kirby and J.D. had arrived at the Szabo home, her third appointment in a busy day, and she'd sent J.D. to the neighbor's house with Anna's two children. He'd delivered foals and calves, even watched a litter of his grandfather's pigs being born back on the reservation, but none of that had prepared J.D. for the experience of assisting at the birth of a child.

"Come on, honey," J.D. encouraged, wiping Anna's forehead with a damp cloth as she struggled through another contraction. "We're almost there."

Her hand tightened on his and he could almost feel her gathering her strength. When she pushed, she bared her teeth and a low groan rolled up from her throat.

J.D. looked expectantly at Kirby, who was supervising the birth from the foot of the bed.

"That's the way." She reached forward, a broad smile on her face. "Anna, it's a boy."

Anna fell back onto the bed. "Is he okay?" she gasped, voice ragged with fatigue. She must have been scared when she went into labor with no one here but her other children.

"Looks fine," Kirby replied, working busily.

J.D. was caught off guard by the rush of emotion that filled him when she held up the squirming infant and placed him on his mother's stomach, cord still attached. The birth process never failed to move J.D., and this time was no exception. He felt tremendous respect for Kirby, who'd taken total control of the situation by the time he'd gotten back from the neighbor's. She must have delivered dozens of babies.

"He's beautiful," Anna murmured, touching his red, wrinkled cheek with her finger.

"He's a handsome fellow," Kirby replied as the infant began to fuss and wave his tiny arms. "Don't you agree, J.D.?"

To him, it was Kirby who was beautiful, even with damp strands of hair clinging to her pale face. "The baby looks perfect," he agreed, experiencing a connection he didn't remember feeling when he'd delivered a foal. Looking at Kirby, he saw an answering softness in her eyes. For a wordless moment, his gaze stayed locked on hers.

"What do those letters in your name stand for?"

Anna asked him, swiveling her head around and breaking the silent connection.

"Why do you want to know?" he demanded suspiciously as Kirby took the baby and dealt with the cord. She had performed hasty introductions when he started assisting her. At the time, the woman had been in so much discomfort that he hadn't thought she really saw him.

"I need a name for my new son," she said now with a touch of pride.

Startled, J.D. glanced at Kirby, who was cleaning up the newest little Szabo. She gave him an approving smile. Unable to think of an excuse, he ducked his head and raked a hand through his hair.

"I was named after James Dean, the actor," he muttered, face flaming. "My mother had a crush on him and she thought his death at such a young age was a tragedy."

"Death is always tragic," Anna replied wearily. "But I like the name. If you don't mind, I'll call this child James Dean Szabo. Has a nice ring to it, don't you think?"

"That it does," Kirby agreed, lips twitching with amusement as she handed the baby, now wrapped in a faded blanket, to his mother.

J.D. sent Kirby a warning glance. He had always been self-conscious about the fancy handle and had gone by the initials since grade school, when his grandpa had suggested the switch, but he didn't really mind that Kirby knew. After today, they shared a bond of sorts as a result of a moving experience. But he'd do well to remember they were still just two people who'd been thrown together—over his objections and his better sense. He didn't dare assume anything more.

Before J.D. could think of anything else to say, they heard the sound of an approaching car.

"That must be your sister, Anna," Kirby said. "I called her on the cell phone when we first got here. She'll stay for a couple of days. J.D., would you go out and see if she needs a hand with anything while I help Anna change?"

"Sure thing." Kirby's eyes went wide as he leaned forward to push several strands of hair off her forehead. "You did a great job," he said, surprising both of them, before he grabbed his hat and walked quickly from the room.

While he was gone, Kirby got Anna into a clean nightgown and changed the bedding.

"My baby's namesake is a man worth hanging on to," Anna said as Kirby dumped the soiled linen in a corner.

"He's just my driver," she explained. "I still don't know my way around very well." She'd told Anna that she was from Idaho.

Before the woman could make another disconcerting remark about J.D., her sister burst into the room and began exclaiming over the baby. When Anna had introduced her, Kirby gave the two women a few brief instructions and filled out some paperwork. After they'd both thanked her several times, and she'd reminded Anna's sister to pick up the other children at the neighbor's, she gave the baby a last hug and left the bedroom.

In the kitchen, J.D. was washing dishes at the sink. Kirby picked up a towel and began drying them. When she put them away in the nearly empty cupboard, the small supply of food there and in the ancient refrigerator dismayed her.

She was thinking about leaving some money for supplies when she saw J.D. slip two twenties from his wallet and tuck them under the corner of a vinyl placemat on the cluttered table. His furtive movements told her he didn't want her to know, so she refrained from commenting on his generosity. Instead she opened the front door and waited for him outside with her medical bag, contemplating what a complex man he was as a few scattered snowflakes swirled around her. He followed her down the steps as she rubbed absently at a cramped muscle in her lower back.

"Backache?" J.D. asked, taking the bag from her hand.

"Just a twinge."

"You must be exhausted." His perception surprised her, and then she realized what she must look like—lip gloss chewed off, mascara smudged, hair a tangled mess. Clothes rumpled and stained. No doubt his concern had been sparked by her bedraggled appearance.

"I'm okay." Her back throbbed dully. "It's been a long day, though. I'll be glad to get home." She turned for a last glance at Anna's modest home. Had she been scared, living out here by herself, without a phone or a decent car? Kirby wondered. At least her sister was with her now.

"It won't be easy for them," J.D. commented, breaking into Kirby's thoughts. "Where's the baby's father?"

"I don't know," Kirby admitted. Anna's file said she was divorced, but gave no details. "Have you ever been married?'' Kirby asked J.D. without thinking.

His eyes narrowed. "No, and I haven't fathered any children and abandoned them, either."

"I didn't think you had."

He merely raised one eyebrow.

After they both got in the Bronco, where the wipers cleared the snowflakes from the windshield, Kirby opted for a change of subject. "Despite everything, you could see the love on Anna's face when she looked at that baby," she mused, thinking of the woman's expression when she saw her new son for the first time, and the way her hand, the skin roughened and red, the nails broken, had gently caressed his blotchy skin.

"I hope that love is enough," J.D. said as he drove around the other car and back out the rutted driveway. His tone said he didn't think it would be.

Kirby recalled the meager furnishings and the peeling floor covering. "So do I." A lump formed in her throat and a headache nagged.

As if he sensed her sudden emotion, J.D. pulled over to the shoulder of the deserted road and killed the engine. "They'll be okay. There's help to be had if she wants it."

"I know." Kirby gulped, silently cursing her inability to remain unaffected by her patients' problems. It was something she'd never really mastered. Her eyes filled at the thought of little James Dean Szabo growing up without the privileges some children took for granted.

Before she could dash the tears away with her fingertips, J.D. thrust a faded red handkerchief at her. For some reason, the gesture undermined the remnants of her control. Turning away, she pressed the folded square against her eyelids and swallowed hard. She took a deep, steadying breath, aware that he'd gotten out—either to give her privacy or to escape her loss of control. She wasn't sure which.

She was still struggling not to cry when her door opened suddenly and she felt the warmth of his hand on her shoulder.

"Come on," he urged. "It will be all right."

Without giving herself time to think, Kirby slid from the seat and went into his waiting arms. The air around them didn't even feel cold.

Shoving aside caution and good sense, J.D. gathered her close. He held her pressed against his chest, absorbing the tremors of emotion rippling through her. Was she aware of the increased thudding of his heart beneath the hand that still clutched his handkerchief?

A sharp surge of desire welled up inside him, shaking him with its intensity as he forced himself to loosen the band of his arms around her. He expected her to push him away the instant she noticed his body's unwilling response to her nearness.

Instead she lifted her head. An answering fire burned in the jade depths of her eyes, and he could no more free her without tasting her lips than he could catch a bird with his bare hands.

An instant before he lowered his head, Kirby read his intent in the sudden tautness of his face. The emotion of the afternoon's events seemed to spin around them, binding them more tightly together, and she gripped the fabric of his shirt to anchor herself. When he hesitated, lips a breath away from hers, she tipped back her head without thinking and closed the tiny gap between them.

She'd have expected his mouth to be hot despite the snow drifting around them, his lips to ravage hers and his tongue to be thrusting and rough. Instead he was achingly gentle, his touch warm and soft, coaxing her to yield so he could explore her with tender strokes of his tongue. Her knees wobbled, threatening to buckle, and her fingers loosened their hold on his shirt, only to tangle in his hair. A moan worked its way up her throat to be trapped in his mouth, and her tongue slid tentatively against his.

When he tasted her response, J.D.'s arms tightened around her and he pressed closer, letting her feel his arousal. The kiss heated, deepened, as her awakening hunger fed his, her hands tightening their hold, her fingers raking the heavy silk of his hair, her body crowding close to his pulsating strength.

Only when she felt him start to pull away, his mouth lingering for one last taste before freeing hers, his eyes smoldering like black fire, did her own responses begin to subside. Heart hammering, she forced her fingers to release his hair, braced herself on her trembling legs as he eased her gently away.

"I didn't mean to do that." His voice was low and harsh.

Shaking her head, Kirby pressed her fingers to his lips. "Don't," she implored, hating the idea that he might apologize for something that felt so right to her.

He wrapped his fingers around her wrist as if to yank her hand away. His gaze searched her face. Then he thrilled her by cupping his other hand around her chin and swooping close again. This time the kiss was brief, hard, and left her lips tingling. After he released her, he didn't smile, but he did loop one arm across her shoulders.

"Let's go home," he said gruffly. "It's been a long day and this weather is supposed to get worse."

Kirby hesitated and he dropped his arm. "I wish we could go home, but I've got two more patients to visit before I'm done." She was surprised that her voice sounded so normal. What she wanted was a few minutes alone to sort out the feelings racing through her.

"Either one of them an emergency?" he asked, after they'd gotten back in the Bronco and he'd turned the key in the ignition.

"Just routine, I think." Doing her best to follow his lead and pretend that nothing earthshaking had just happened between them, she flipped open the files and scanned their contents. "Nothing urgent."

"Reschedule them," he told her as he pulled back onto the road. "You're beat and it sounds as though they could both wait."

"Good idea. Let's go home." She looked at him, but his expression didn't appear to have changed any since he'd kissed her. She wondered if that had merely been part of his attempt to comfort her, and she hated the thought.

"How many babies have you delivered?" he asked when she was done calling on the cellular phone. "You barely broke a sweat."

"This is the first time I've delivered one on my own," she admitted, relieved that the birth had been routine. "I'm used to having a doctor present."

"Good thing the mother didn't know that," he replied. A slight smile edged his lips as he slowed behind a car that was poking down the road.

"I couldn't have done as well without your help," she told him sincerely. "I'm glad you were with me."

For a moment, his gaze met hers and she wondered if he, too, was thinking of the kiss they'd shared.

"You did good in there," he said.

Her breath caught in her throat. Before she could formulate a reply, he pulled out and passed the other car. "So did you," she said. "I was surprised."

"Did you expect me to faint or just refuse to help you?" he asked.

His tone made her smile. "I'm glad you did neither, but I've seen fathers panic, and they've attended classes." While he'd been coaching Anna, he'd managed to distract her from the pain with questions about her other two children. Kirby had never heard him talk so much before, and she'd seen a side to him that she hadn't anticipated. "You can help me with a delivery anytime," she told him.

He shrugged, as if her gratitude made him uneasy. "It's not that different from midwifing a broodmare, and I've had plenty of practice at that. If you're still here in the spring when they start dropping foals, perhaps you can return the favor."

"I'd like that." Delighted with the idea that he might want her help, she smiled at him, but he kept his attention on the road ahead. His face was settled into its habitual distant expression, making her wonder whether it had really been him kissing her so passionately or if she had fallen asleep and dreamed the whole thing.

Damn, J.D. thought. What had he been doing, kissing Kirby like that?

Restlessly, he urged Buck forward as he dragged

in a lungful of cold, crisp air and scanned the horizon. The ranchland was patchy with the snow that had been falling sporadically. He'd been up all night with a sick horse and had just left the vet, who'd pronounced the colt well out of danger.

Buchanan would be relieved; Fancy Pants was a promising stud for which he'd dropped a bundle. For once, J.D. didn't care about the horse, didn't care about the job he needed as much as he resented the reasons behind it.

All he could think about was the sound Kirby had made, deep in her throat, when he'd taken her mouth. He'd meant to grind it under his in desperate frustration, but the touch of her lips had affected him in an unexpected way, making him want to give instead of take.

Not that he'd ever been purposely selfish. When making love to a woman, he'd always tried to bring her pleasure even as he sought his own. Heat seeped through him when he remembered the way Kirby had tasted and how she yielded to him, opening her mouth so he could possess it more fully.

With a fierce surge of hunger, his body reacted to the images flooding his mind.

For once, J.D. was dangerously close to questioning the creed he'd adopted after his accident, the desire to regain his independence—to need no one's help or pity. How sweet it would be to lose himself in the embrace of a soft, sweet woman like Kirby, and how destructive when she realized he had nothing left to give.

Everything that mattered had already been stripped from him. The only thing he had left was his sense of self, and he'd be damned if he'd lose that as well.

Still, when he recognized the lone rider off to the right, he turned Buck's head in that direction, unable to deny himself.

Kirby spotted the other rider before she could hear his hoofbeats. When he was still too far away to recognize, she reined in Duke and waited to see if he was headed her way. Before she left, she had told Bobbie she'd be riding south. Had something happened back at the house? Just the other day, Bobbie had mentioned how reassuring it was to have a trained nurse on the Rocking Rose in case of any emergency that might come up.

Something about the way the rider sat his horse was familiar. As soon as she could tell that the mount was light colored, Kirby's heart began to pound. She hadn't seen J.D. since the afternoon he'd kissed her. The ride back to the ranch had been anticlimactic after that; neither of them referred to what had happened at Anna's, but it had stayed between them all the same. At least it stayed in *her* mind.

Perhaps it meant no more to J.D. than scratching an itch, and he'd forgotten all about it. How Kirby wished she could do the same.

Now she resisted the urge to dig her heels into Duke's sides and send him racing away. Curiosity and her own stubborn refusal to run kept her still. That and the desire to see J.D. again.

"I thought that was you," he said when he came within shouting distance.

"How did you know?"

He pointed to her head, which was bare in deference to the late fall sunshine. She'd stuffed one of

Donovan's baseball caps in her pocket, but she hadn't wanted to put it on.

"Your hair's like a beacon," he added, reining in Buck so the horses were nose-to-tail.

"Were you looking for me? Is anything wrong?"

He shook his head without indicating which of her questions he was answering. Then he turned his mount and began to amble companionably through the dead and yellowed grass.

Without any signal from Kirby, Duke started walking alongside Buck. "You aren't working this morning," she said, then bit her tongue at the inane remark. Would he think she was criticizing him?

"I was up all night with one of the horses," he explained, and she noticed for the first time the dark smudges beneath his eyes. "This morning the vet gave the okay, so I decided to clear out the cobwebs." He gestured toward his head, covered as usual by his black Stetson.

"I'm glad the horse is better. I know that Donovan's been worried."

"He spent the last couple of nights in the stable. He would have been there last night, too, if he wasn't almost out on his feet."

For a few moments they rode without speaking, the only sounds the creak of saddle leather, the soft thud of horses' hooves and the occasional cry of a bird overhead. Since J.D. had started driving her on her rounds, Kirby had grown used to his silences. Even when he was quiet, she didn't feel ill at ease. Or at least she hadn't until that kiss. Now she wasn't so sure.

"You ride nearly every day," J.D. commented suddenly.

"Is that okay? I didn't mean to monopolize Duke if someone else needs him," Kirby replied.

Donovan had told her she could take him out whenever she felt like it, that the ranch hands had their own mounts. But she didn't want to inconvenience anyone.

J.D. waved his hand dismissively. "It's no problem. Your riding's improving. You've got a natural seat."

She flushed at the unexpected compliment. Today the blue plaid shirt that was visible under his open jacket complemented his deeply bronzed skin, although she would have bet he never noticed. The long muscles of his thighs strained against the faded denim of his jeans and his gloved hands held the reins with easy competence.

"Where did you learn so much about horses?" Kirby asked when he didn't say anything else. She half expected him to ignore her question.

Instead, he surprised her by shifting in the saddle so he could face her and slowing Buck's gait even further with a touch of the reins.

"My grandfather was a horse whisperer. He passed his knowledge on to me."

The term intrigued her. "What's a horse whisperer do?" she asked.

J.D. searched her face as if he was reassuring himself of her interest. "Basically, it's an ancient method of gentling horses by talking softly to them until their fears are calmed. That's probably simplifying it some, though."

"It sounds nice," she said. "Much better than breaking their spirits with brute force." She wanted to ask him more questions, like how he'd become a rodeo rider, but she hesitated to disturb the tentative new bond between them.

"My grandfather was Navajo," he said, looking straight ahead so his face was in profile. "But my mother was half-white."

"You must have loved your grandfather very much," she guessed. J.D.'s voice had softened when he spoke of him.

He considered for a moment. "I did. His name was Chee Whitehorse. My mother and I lived with him down on the rez for a while when I was a kid. He got pneumonia and died a few years back."

"I'm sorry." Kirby wasn't sure what else to say, but she wasn't going to let the conversation end when he was in such a talkative mood. "What led you to rodeoing?" she finally ventured.

He glanced at her and shrugged. "It was a way to make money, first in Indian rodeos and then PRCA. When I was a kid, someone was always trying to stay on the back of some critter or another. Got so it would turn into a contest to see who could stick the longest."

From watching it on television, she knew the Professional Rodeo Cowboys' Association was the biggest and most successful of the organizations. "Donovan told me you were good, a natural."

For a moment his face relaxed and he must have been remembering. "Yeah," he drawled, "I was pretty good, but your brother was better. He was always ahead of me."

"He told me you might have beaten him if you hadn't been hurt." As soon as she mentioned the accident, she knew it was a mistake.

His expression grew bleak and she knew the odd

moments of companionship were over. "We'd better get back," he said as he turned his horse's head. Without looking to see if she was behind him, he urged Buck into a trot.

Musing over what he'd told her as she watched him sit his horse so effortlessly, Kirby followed him back to the stable. If anything, the little he'd told her had only made her more curious about him.

"Good news," Buchanan said as he rested one foot on the fence rail and watched J.D. work a yearling filly on a lunge line.

J.D. looked up as Buchanan pushed back the brim of his hat. "Yeah?" He went back to working the filly, a yearling named Popcorn he was buying from Buchanan. When J.D. had her thoroughly gentled, he planned to sell her and buy two more. Not only was Buchanan content to take a monthly payment out of J.D.'s wages, he didn't seem to begrudge him the time he spent with her as long as his other work didn't suffer.

More guilt, J.D. had decided. Now he wasn't so sure. Just the other day, Buchanan had offered to include the filly in his own spring sale if she was ready. J.D. knew he'd get a better price working with Buchanan than he would selling her on his own. He couldn't figure the other man out, but if it was indeed guilt that motivated him, he must be carrying around a pile of it.

"Charlie got a clean bill of health this morning. He can take over driving Kirby next time."

They were the words J.D. had been waiting to hear, especially since he'd lost it the other day and kissed her. Now he wanted to say it was about time, but he couldn't seem to get the words out.

Leading his filly to the paddock gate, he glanced at Buchanan and then began fiddling with the latch. In his opinion, Charlie Babcock was a strong kid, but he had the sense of a dung beetle. In an emergency, there was no saying whether he'd be any real help, let alone capable of assisting in anything as serious as the birth of a baby.

"Forget that," he said as surprise crossed Buchanan's face. "If Charlie's ready to go back to work, let him clean stalls while I play chauffeur. I've got the time, it's easy work and it all pays the same."

"Makes no difference to me," Buchanan replied with a grin. "And Kirby seems to think you have natural talent as a midwife."

J.D. released the breath he'd been holding. It wasn't as if he was worried about Charlie getting out of line, but why should J.D. bend his back over a pitchfork when he didn't have to?

He'd taken Popcorn through the gate and was about to lead her over to the stable when Buchanan cleared his throat. Bracing himself for an argument, J.D. waited as the filly pranced at his side.

"Kirby's been through a lot of emotional turmoil lately," Buchanan told him. "I don't think she's really dealt with the idea that she was adopted."

J.D. remembered how upset she'd been that night he found her outside his house. She hadn't mentioned it since. Was Buchanan looking for some kind of assurance or fishing to see what she'd told J.D.?

"I guess it would be difficult, finding out you're not who you thought you were," he said slowly. "She's a strong woman, though. She'll sort it out."

"You're probably right," Buchanan agreed, coming over to run a hand down the filly's back.

J.D. watched him with growing suspicion. He usually had no trouble making a point; J.D. had seen him light into more than one ranch hand he thought had a problem with hard work. "Is that all?" he asked bluntly. "'Cause if it is, I got things to do."

For a moment, Buchanan merely studied him, making J.D. wonder if he had dirt on his face. Then his jaw bunched. "She's vulnerable," he said. "I don't want her hurt."

It took J.D. a second to sort out what the boss was getting at. When he did, anger made him grip the filly's lead tighter, to avoid shoving a fist under Buchanan's nose.

"If you're worried I'll take advantage of her between nursing calls, you'd better find another driver," he said through clenched teeth. Then his conscience rose up and bit him. Had Kirby told her brother that he'd kissed her? Would she have confided that kind of thing to him, or perhaps to his wife? If she had a problem, she'd damn well better come straight to him with it.

"I've never laid a hand on a woman who didn't want it," he said aloud. The memory of her response whipped through him. Had she allowed it because she was *vulnerable,* for pity's sake? The idea made him furious, although he wasn't sure why.

"Let's just forget the whole damn thing," he told Buchanan. "I'm sure Charlie's hormones are under much better control than mine."

"Confound it, J.D.," Buchanan began, blocking his way when he would have pushed by. "You know I wasn't accusing you of anything, but a woman can get the wrong idea sometimes, especially if she's been through a raw time emotionally. I wanted you to be on your guard, that's all.''

Before J.D. could reply, a feminine voice asked briskly, ''And just what, exactly, are you cautioning poor Mr. Reese to be on his guard against?''

Chapter Seven

Wearing matching expressions of dismay, Donovan and J.D. turned around to gape at Kirby, who was standing in the aisle of the stable with her hands braced on her hips. The two men, she decided, looked exactly like little boys caught putting a snake in someone's lunch box.

"Hi, sis." Donovan's voice had a falsely hearty tone that only served to increase her suspicion.

J.D.'s smile was equally as counterfeit. "Hey, city girl."

Donovan's brows rose. "She's from Boise," he commented.

"I know that."

"I asked what you were warning J.D. about," she repeated, as Donovan twiddled the ends of his mustache between his thumb and forefinger. The gesture, she'd noticed before, was one he sometimes resorted to when he needed a moment to collect his thoughts.

"Was I warning him about something?" Donovan asked. He turned to J.D. "Do you remember some sort of a warning?"

J.D. shrugged. "Beats me."

Why was it, when confronted by a woman, two men who could be sworn enemies invariably banded together like blood brothers? she wondered.

"I heard you," she said, resisting the urge to tap her foot.

Donovan's eyes widened innocently. "You did?" he echoed.

Kirby's patience began to fray like a cheap carpet. "I'm waiting."

"I'll leave you to deal with this," J.D. told her brother. "As far as that other business goes, I got your message loud and clear," he said enigmatically. "Have it your way, and don't bother talking to Charlie." Touching the brim of his hat in a gesture that Kirby would have bet money was purely automatic, he turned and stalked away.

Donovan walked over and gave her a hug. "So, how are you?" he asked, flashing his dimples.

"Still curious," she replied, refusing to be side-tracked. "Why do I have the feeling that you two were discussing me?"

He seemed genuinely baffled. "You do?" Then his face cleared. "You must have overheard us talking about a horse we're training for a neighbor," he said, his gaze not quite meeting hers.

Kirby stepped closer and searched his face for any sign of deception. "You were warning J.D. about something."

Donovan scratched the side of his neck. "Was I?" His frown was thoughtful. "Oh, I must have been telling him that the colt likes to buck. That's why Harry's sending him over, so J.D. can teach him some manners."

"Uh-huh." Kirby was still unconvinced. J.D. hadn't looked as if they were discussing horses. He'd been scowling when she walked up on them.

"What is it now?" Donovan demanded, a note of righteous indignation in his voice. "You don't believe me? What else could we have been discussing? Do you think I was warning him away from you, because you're so man hungry?"

Now Kirby had to smile. He had a point, and she was being needlessly paranoid. "I guess not," she admitted. "You'd hardly need to warn J.D. about me when the last thing on my mind is men." Lord, but she hoped her nose didn't grow! That kiss she'd shared with J. D. Reese was just about the only thing she'd been able to think about, but she was hardly about to admit that to her matchmaking brother.

"By the way," Donovan added as if he'd just remembered, "Charlie is going to be busy working in the stable for a while, so unless you have any objections, J.D. will continue to drive you when the weather's bad, at least."

Kirby had to smother a pleased smile. Not only did she find the trainer extremely attractive, but he exuded a quiet confidence she trusted to get them through any situation that might arise. Perhaps he didn't have a lot to say, but she was determined to draw him out as they continued to work together.

"No problem," she said airily. "He seems to know

his way around well enough and he can certainly change a tire.''

Had Donovan's eyes narrowed slightly? "Right," he said dryly. "The man's a real wonder."

It was Kirby's turn to raise her eyebrows in silent inquiry, but he didn't say anything more. After he'd excused himself and headed down to the bunkhouse, she mulled over his last remark. It had come across as slightly sarcastic. How *did* the two men feel about each other, anyway? Theirs was certainly a relationship brought about by unusual circumstances. Would they have been friends otherwise? Probably not. From what her brother had told her, they'd never had much to do with each other on the bull-riding circuit.

Not that Donnie was implying anything now, though. She just had to quit leaping to conclusions, that was all.

Kirby reminded herself of that same thing several times during the next few days as she visited patients while J.D. waited in the Bronco. If the kiss they had shared entered his mind at all, it probably stirred nothing more complicated than mild regret. Except for being only slightly less aloof than before, he hadn't changed his behavior toward her one whit.

J.D. did regret kissing her, only the feeling was anything but mild. He regretted it bitterly. His nights were haunted by the memory of her taste on his lips, and sitting next to her in the cab of the Bronco without being able to reach over and touch her whenever he felt like it was sheer torture. On more than one occasion he'd come too damned close to pulling over to the shoulder of the road and finding out if kissing her was half as good as he remembered.

Even half as good would have been pretty damned spectacular.

If he hadn't been so busy fighting the temptation one late afternoon when he was driving her on her rounds, he might have noticed just how severe the storm brewing since that morning had grown. Although the temperature was up after the recent cold spell, rain had been falling steadily for hours and now strong winds lashed the truck.

The visit Kirby had just completed—cleaning and changing the dressing on an elderly woman's foot after she'd had surgery on her toes—had taken three times as long as it should have. Kirby hadn't liked the looks of one of the incisions and had waited an hour for the doctor to return her call. That delay, added to one in the morning when the Bronco wouldn't start and they'd had to take an old ranch pickup instead, had put them way behind schedule.

Now tall, angry clouds surged across the darkening sky and the wind kicked leaves and small branches in their path on the narrow dirt track they'd been following for the past half hour. The rain had increased from a mere downpour to a deluge, beating against the windshield so hard that J.D. had to focus all his attention on the portion of road lit by their headlights in order to keep from missing a curve and getting stuck in the soft mud.

Seated next to him, Kirby seemed unaffected by the storm boiling up around them. Until a couple of moments before, she'd been chattering about one of Taylor's dogs, named Tramp, and how he liked to play Frisbee with her nephews.

"I think we must have taken a wrong turn back there," J.D. muttered, swerving to miss a branch that blew into their path. As he spun the wheel, the truck began to fishtail. Swearing under his breath, he corrected the skid. "I should have thrown some weight in the back. The road's getting narrower. If the rain gets any worse, it'll turn to mud and we'll have to head back."

"If you think that's best." She peered out the window as if she'd just noticed the weather. She'd been preoccupied today and he wondered what was on her mind.

Another gust shook the pickup and he slowed even further. "Did your directions say anything about that shack we passed? It looked abandoned." He flipped on the interior light, and Kirby squinted at the paper she held in her hand.

"No mention of a building," she replied. "We should have gone by a tall burned stump on the left before now. Is it possible that we missed it?"

"I don't think so, but anything's possible, I guess." His imagination tormented him with images of her soaking wet from the rain, her clothes clinging to her curves, the fabric translucent and her nipples beaded from the cold. He could picture the water dripping from the ends of her hair, running in rivulets down her neck to pool in the hollow at the base of her throat, and he thought about licking it—

A rabbit ran in front of the truck and he stabbed at the brake.

"How far have we gone?" she asked as he wrestled with the wheel. "The house is supposed to be only a little over seven miles off the main road."

J.D. glanced at the odometer. "We've gone farther than that already." He looked around, but the storm had reduced visibility dramatically.

"Maybe we should turn back," Kirby suggested, absently nibbling her lower lip as J.D.'s mouth watered. How well he remembered the satiny feel of that lip.

Rain battered the pickup. Already hitting the windshield like a thousand tiny pebbles, it seemed to double in volume.

"That does it," J.D. said, easing on the brake until he felt the wheels grab. "We'll come back tomorrow if the weather's better." Carefully, he maneuvered the truck forward, looking for a wide spot in which to turn around. His hopes weren't high; there'd been no turnouts since they'd passed the shack.

Finally, as the ground grew softer and sucked at the tires, he stopped again. "Do you think, if I direct you, that you could turn the truck around without getting stuck?" he asked, opening his door. Immediately, a wall of water blew in, drenching the side of his face and neck. "Just slide over behind the wheel."

"You'll get soaked," she protested.

"Can't be helped. It's too dark out there to see the edge of the road, such as it is." He looked at her expectantly.

Kirby angled her chin and her eyes sparkled. "I'll do my best."

"That's all either of us can do." J.D. leaned across her to get the flashlight from the glove box. Glancing up, he hesitated, so near to her he could see his own reflection in her pupils. He swayed closer. As soon as he realized what he was doing, he grabbed the flashlight and scrambled from the pickup so fast that he almost slipped and fell.

The road was as slick as the back of a greased pig. His bad hip twisted painfully as he shifted his weight

heavily in an effort to keep his balance. The full force
of the storm hit, nearly ripping his hat from his head,
and he silently berated himself. Fool! He should have
insisted they start back when he'd first sensed the road
wasn't the one described in Kirby's directions.

Cautiously, Kirby worked the clutch as she did her
best to follow the beam of the flashlight in the unre-
lenting gloom. She wished she could see J.D.'s expression, but his face through the streaked glass was
only a pale blur.

Longing for her Bronco, she backed the old truck
slowly down the narrow track, hitting the brake harder
than she'd intended when he finally made a chopping
motion with the light. The engine died, he shouted
and the steering wheel jumped in her hands as she
felt the pickup buck abruptly.

Before she could react, J.D. was at her door.

"I'm sorry," she exclaimed. "It's been a while
since I drove a stick shift."

His expression was grim. "Slide over."

Quickly, she did as he'd asked. "Are we stuck?"

Hunched over the wheel, he turned the key. Rain
dripped off the brim of his Stetson and darkened the
denim of his jacket, turning it black in the glow from
the cab light. His face was wet, his lashes matted
together.

"We're in mud to the hubs," he replied, easing the
truck into gear. While Kirby waited silently, scarcely
daring to breathe, he did his best to free them. When
the wheels continued to spin he got back out, telling
her to stay put.

"No point in both of us getting soaked," he added
before he disappeared into the darkness.

Ignoring his orders, she followed him, dismayed at the force of the rain stinging her cheeks like tiny whips. When he scowled at her, she took the flashlight and held it while he packed what branches he could find under the wheels. When they tried again, the truck still refused to break loose of its gluey prison.

"I wish I hadn't forgotten the phone," Kirby lamented in a small voice, hardly daring to distract him. She'd left it in the Bronco that morning.

"No kidding." Twice more they climbed back out and fiddled with the branches. The second time, she noticed that he was limping badly.

"You hurt yourself," she said when they were back inside.

He shrugged. "Slipped in the mud. No big deal."

She knew his pride would never allow him to favor his hip unless he was in nearly unbearable pain, but she didn't say anything more. If need be, she could take the light and walk to the main road.

Finally, J.D. shut off the engine and sat back, staring through the windshield with a grim expression. Mud streaked his cheek and clung to his boots. His hands were red and his face was pale.

Kirby was unable to suppress a sneeze.

"Are you wet through?" he asked.

Lightly, she touched his shoulder. His jacket had to be soaked. "Not as bad as you," she replied as a hard shiver rippled through him.

"We'll have to hike back to that shack we passed," he said as if he were thinking aloud. "It wasn't that far and we'll be more comfortable there. When it's light, I'll look for a shovel, a board, anything to dig the wheels out with."

"When it's light?" she echoed. "You mean to-morrow morning?"

His stare was hooded. "I didn't plan this, you know."

Kirby felt her cheeks flush as she realized how he'd taken her protest. "I only meant that Donovan and Bobbie will be worried when I don't show up," she explained. "I didn't think—"

"Never mind," he cut in. "I was out of line."

He slapped the steering wheel with his wet hand. Tentatively, she touched his bare wrist below the sleeve of his jacket. His skin was icy cold.

"It's okay," she said. "I'll walk out to the main road and get help."

His head swung around and he gaped at her. "Have you lost your mind?"

Kirby tried to make allowances for his tone of voice. He must be tired and discouraged. He was in pain. "No, I don't think so," she said evenly. "But your hip—"

He bared his teeth. "My hip is just dandy. And you can forget about going anywhere alone in this storm." A gust of wind rocked the truck as if it were a child's toy and a new burst of rain rattled against the windows like buckshot.

Kirby set her jaw. Why did men have to be so hardheaded in the face of simple reason? "I think my going makes the most sense," she insisted.

"You don't get a vote." His eyes were narrowed and a muscle jumped in his lean cheek, giving him an edge of danger she would have found wildly attractive under different circumstances.

For some reason, her mind darted back to that kiss they'd shared, and she wondered how anyone so pigheaded could have unbent enough to swamp her senses the way he had. "I beg your pardon," she huffed, leaning away from him. "You're my driver. You work for me."

His lips twitched, annoying her further. "Beg all you want. I work for your brother and he'd have my butt if I let you do a fool thing like that."

She was about to make an angry protest of his assessment. Before she could start, he sighed and his shoulders slumped wearily. "Look," he said in a more reasonable tone, "it's dark and there's no guarantee anyone would drive by in this storm if you did get to the road, which has to be nine miles or better from here. My hip *is* bothering me. There's no way I could make it that far, not tonight. If you sprained an ankle or ran into any other trouble, I couldn't even come looking for you. I'd have no way of knowing. On the other hand, when it's light, I'll probably be able to dig the truck out. By then, the storm will more than likely have moved on or blown itself out."

She knew he had to be desperate to admit to human limitations, and what he said made sense. She looked out the window at the darkness, now absolute. She wasn't eager to walk those miles alone at night, anyway. If need be, she could do it in the morning. It wasn't as if she was afraid to be alone with him; she wasn't. If things were different, she'd enjoy it.

"Can you make it to the cabin?" she asked.

His face relaxed. "I can make it. I just hope there's some wood for a fire. We'll both be soaked through by the time we get there and I don't have to warn you about hypothermia."

"You're right," she said, realizing the possible seriousness of their situation for the first time. "Let's go before it gets any colder."

In a few moments they'd gathered up everything they thought they'd need—Kirby's nursing bag and the food left over from their hasty lunch as well as the emergency kit all the ranch vehicles carried and an old jacket J.D. found behind the seat. They locked the pickup, even though he seemed amused by her insisting they do so, and began the trek back down the road.

In moments, Kirby's parka and jeans were wet. At least her feet, in sturdy boots, were dry. She slipped several times, glad J.D. was there in case she fell. She let him set the pace as he illuminated their way with the flashlight. It seemed to take forever before he finally stopped and shined the light on the cabin squatting in the darkness.

"Home at last," he said lightly.

"What if the door's locked?" she asked.

The flashlight beam hit a small, dirty window. She could see that a corner of the glass was missing and a rag had been jammed into the hole.

"A locked door isn't going to stop us tonight." His voice was determined, filling her with confidence. As long as he was here, they'd both be all right. She was sure of it.

The door was unlocked, but the cabin wasn't much to look at. Their light revealed a single room furnished with a table, four chairs, one of which was broken, a tiny kitchen area with a sink and a gas range, and a cot shoved against the opposite wall. Most important, a pot-bellied stove sat in the far corner near another door.

The first thing J.D. did was to shake the old lantern

that hung over the table. When it made a sloshing noise, he turned up the wick and struck a match. The lamp gave off a glow that made the room appear almost cozy.

"I saw a woodpile outside. Some of it should be dry," J.D. said as he shouldered his way back through the door, taking the flashlight with him.

While he was gone, Kirby noticed faded curtains at the windows, a cupboard on the kitchen wall and an icebox near the sink. She crossed the bare floor and opened the other door cautiously, not wanting to disturb any small critters. Instead, she was delighted to find a little bathroom with two fixtures. The sink was stained with rust and grime, but there was a full roll of paper under a coffee can on the back of the toilet.

Moments after she came back out, J.D. returned, cradling a stack of wood and kindling in one arm. "There's plenty more where this came from," he said. "Most of it's protected by a tarp. The water tank seems full, too."

While he started a fire in the woodstove, Kirby checked the kitchen for supplies. As she opened the empty refrigerator, her stomach rumbled.

"There's no food," she told him, disappointed. "Not even a can of beans."

"The propane tank's empty, as well, so the stove won't work," he replied as he built the fire. "It's a good thing we've got leftovers from lunch." He indicated one of the bags they'd brought with them. While he nursed the flames to life, she laid out crackers, cheese and sugar cookies, then poured two cups of coffee she was pleased to see still gave off a wisp of steam.

He'd taken off his wet jacket, so she hung it and her own over two of the chairs near the stove. Her flannel shirt was barely damp, but she could see that J.D.'s was soaked through. She couldn't help but stare as he straightened and unsnapped it. He freed the tails and peeled the shirt off, revealing rangy but muscular shoulders and arms. Next came his T-shirt, as Kirby watched helplessly. Tufts of black hair grew under his arms.

Something fluttered in her chest when she saw his bare back, the wide expanse halved by the curve of his spine, which disappeared into his jeans. Then she noticed the puckering scar. Her stomach lurched. The angry line started beneath one shoulder blade and curved around to disappear near his ribs. She must have made a sound of dismay, because he turned to face her, holding his T-shirt in both hands.

His chest was roped with muscle and free of hair. In the still-chilly room, his small, dark nipples were drawn into tight nubs. His jeans rode low on his hips, fastened by a wide silver buckle. A faint line of hair disappeared behind it.

She swallowed and her gaze crept up to collide with his. For a long, silent moment, he returned her stare, the expression in his shadowed eyes unreadable. Then a piece of wood in the stove popped loudly, making her jump.

Still watching her, he tossed the T-shirt to a chair and reached up to untie the thong holding back his hair. He raked his fingers through the gleaming strands, freeing them, as his gaze traveled the length of her assessingly, heating her body as it went.

"Your jeans are wet," he said calmly. "Better take them off and hang them by the stove."

"Oh, no, that—that's okay," she stammered, blinking. "I poured some coffee. We'd better drink it while it's still hot."

"Ah, good." Briefly, his mouth curved into a smile as he picked up one of the cups, tipped back his head and took a long drink.

Feeling totally out of her depth, Kirby watched the muscles of his throat work as he swallowed. With a rough sigh of pleasure, he set the cup back down on the table and wiped his mouth on his forearm.

"You'd better drink yours before it gets cold," he observed. "Then get out of those wet clothes."

Automatically, her arms crossed in front of her chest. "My shirt isn't wet."

"It looks wet. If you're worried about your modesty, you can wrap yourself in the blanket from the cot. Don't worry, I'll turn around until you do." He spun away, leaving her to stare again at his broad back.

"Where did you get that scar?" she asked, wincing at the cruel line of it.

"A bull gored me." From the tone of his voice, he might as well have been telling her that a kitten had scratched him.

"How awful."

He glanced over his shoulder, gaze hooded. "Drink your coffee and get your clothes off," he said again, as if he were speaking to a child. "Or I'll have to help you."

She'd been reaching for her cup, but at his words her gaze flew back to his. He arched a brow and one corner of his mouth lifted. Bare chested, with his hair hanging loose around his face, he looked both exotic and infinitely attractive.

Kirby's hand shook as she reached for the coffee, and it sloshed over the rim, stinging her skin.

She gasped, and he caught the cup as she let it go. Before she could protest, he dragged her toward the sink and ran cold water on the burn. Then he pulled her closer to the light from the lantern and examined her hand.

"Still hurt?" he asked. "It's only a little pink."

She tugged free of his grip as his eyes narrowed. "No, the coffee isn't that hot. It just startled me." She was annoyed that her voice was shaking, but she hoped he hadn't noticed.

Obviously, he had. When she started to go around him, intent on sitting down at the table, he shifted abruptly and blocked her path. Her gaze settled on his chest and froze there.

He was beautifully made, lean and muscular, his smooth skin bathed bronze by the light from the kerosene lamp. Suddenly, his chest expanded as he sighed heavily.

"I see there's one thing we need to take care of before we can go on," he said in a resigned voice.

Had he spotted a mouse or a spider? "What's that?" she asked with a frown, looking around.

"This." He lifted his hands and closed them over her shoulders. Then he gave a tug, pulling her closer. She lost her balance and her palms flattened against his chest. His skin was surprisingly warm. While she stared up at him, wide-eyed with shock, he bent his head and his fingers flexed on her shoulders. "You're right," he murmured, just before his mouth closed over hers. "Your shirt is nearly dry."

Chapter Eight

When Kirby felt J.D.'s tongue brush her lips, seeking entrance, passion swamped her common sense. With a tiny moan, she yielded, welcoming him. Beneath the hand she'd pressed to his bare chest she could feel the steady thud of his heart. Hers was thundering like stampeding cattle.

His arms clamped her tighter, and his mouth moved over hers with increasing urgency. Desire, hot and sweet, whipped through her. He smelled of rain and wind, elemental and untamed. She slid her arms around his neck and pressed herself against him, glorying when she felt a hard shudder rack his body.

Dragging in a tortured breath, he slid his knee between her thighs and leaned into her feminine warmth. His hand glided down her back and his fingers splayed across her hip, anchoring her close. She could feel his arousal. Her breasts flattened against the expanse of his chest, her nipples tightening into sensitive nubs.

A ragged groan worked its way up from deep in his throat as he finally tore his mouth from hers.

"J.D." she pleaded, tightening her hold around his neck.

She felt him stiffen, felt his hands on her arms as he tried to detach her. Desperate, she pressed her mouth to the side of his neck, where a pulse throbbed. She inhaled his scent, tasted the tang of his skin.

He bent his head and captured her mouth in another searing kiss as her breathing thinned and her brain emptied. His tongue tangled with hers. His hands, more urgent now, stroked her arms, clasped her waist. Gently, he cupped her breast, thumb teasing the nipple. With a sigh, she pressed against him.

Over and over, he kissed her. Reaching blindly, she buried her fingers in his silky hair. Like a big cat seeking her caress, he rubbed his head against her palm and a purr rumbled in his throat.

He framed her face with his hands and his mouth ravaged hers. Slowly, she felt herself sinking in a sea of desire, her blood running hot, her breathing reduced to shallow puffs of air. Her knees were weak, her arms heavy. Her hands shook. Around the cabin, the wind howled, shaking the walls. She was barely aware of it.

With a suddenness that shocked her, he grabbed her wrists and jerked her away. His chest heaved, his breath rasping. His eyes were narrowed to slits and passion honed his face, throwing his cheekbones into sharp relief.

"You test me," he groaned, voice thick. "You

tempt me. What are you thinking, letting me do this?''

Her eyes went wide. ''You wanted—I thought...'' Staring into his hard face, she stumbled and stuttered, confused.

He took a step back from her and raked his fingers through his hair. She was gratified to see that his hand trembled ever so slightly. The sight of that tiny weakness gave her courage.

''I wanted to kiss you,'' she whispered. ''And you wanted to kiss me.''

''And do you always give men what they want?'' he asked.

She gasped as hurt plunged into her like the point of a knife.

''I'm sorry.'' He bent his head. ''I should never have said that.'' He extended his hand, palm upward.

Still reeling from the abrupt change in him, she stared at his hand but made no move to take it.

With a bitter oath, he whirled away, grabbed his jacket and shrugged into it as he crossed the room with long, uneven strides.

''Where are you going?'' she cried, contrite.

''I've got to get out of here before I do something we'll both regret.''

Perhaps his words should have frightened her, but as the door of the shack slammed behind him, she felt only a burning regret that he'd left. Sinking into a chair by the fire, she touched her fingers to her swollen lips and willed him to come back to her.

Outside, J.D. tilted back his bare head and let the rain beat down on his face while the cold air chilled his skin and cooled his overheated blood. What the hell had he been thinking, going at her like an animal?

She should have been repulsed by his crude assault. Even though she had said she wanted his kiss, perhaps she'd been too scared to resist, alone with him in the middle of nowhere. Like a fist to the gut, the thought that he might have frightened her nearly doubled him over. Gasping, he braced his hand against the wall and hung his head, dragging in deep breaths until his lungs burned and his heart hammered in his chest.

God! The possibility made him want to sink to his knees and howl with shame. Tearing himself away from the wall, he jammed his shaking hands into the pockets of his jacket and walked down the road, into the night.

He stumbled once, the pain that shot through his hip nearly tripping him, and then common sense began to seep into his fevered brain. It was too dark to see. If he fell and injured himself, he'd be useless to Kirby, and she'd need him to dig out the truck in the morning.

His feet slowed and then stopped. Eyes squeezed shut, he let the rain pelt his face like tiny, stinging arrows. Then, when he was finally calm, he turned and carefully retraced his steps.

Back in the shack, Kirby put another log in the stove and stood near it with her arms wrapped around her middle, trying to absorb the warmth of the fire. She was shivering all over.

Had she thrown herself at J.D.? Had he even wanted her? Or did he think she hadn't welcomed his kiss? The questions tore at her like darting piranhas, ripping at her fragile feelings as if they were tiny bites of tender flesh. She was still fighting tears when the door slammed open.

Startled, she spun around as a blast of cold air hit her. One look at J.D.'s tortured expression—at the water streaming from his face and hair—and all thought of her own needs fled.

"You have to get out of those wet clothes," she told him as he shut the door. She reached out to grab his arm and drag him closer to the stove.

While he shrugged wordlessly out of his sodden jacket, she found a frayed, grimy towel on the sink and tried to dry his hair and face. He took it and blotted his neck while she grabbed his shirt from the back of a chair where he'd hung it earlier. It was dry and warm, so she put it around his shoulders.

Before she could take her hands away, he covered them with his.

"I wasn't running from you," he said, voice deep and soft as he turned her around.

She saw the expression in his fathomless eyes and froze. "I know that." Suddenly, she did know. He'd been running from himself.

"I needed...I guess I needed some air," he said with a crooked smile and an endearing shrug. His shirt was still slung across his shoulders, the front hanging open.

Taking a deep breath, Kirby raised her hands and pressed them against his bare chest. She was afraid, terribly afraid, that he'd reject her again. More than the fear, though, was the need, rising inside her, clawing at her. The need to comfort this man who held himself apart, to feel and taste him once again, the need to drink in his scent and stroke the texture of his skin. To bask in his strength and heat, to hold him in her arms and let the excitement rise between them like a riptide.

At the touch of her hand on his skin, he squeezed his eyes shut and drew in a deep, shuddering breath. Then he reached up to link their fingers. Leading her to the cot, his gaze locked on hers, he sat down and tugged gently. As the springs protested, she sat next to him.

"If you want me to stop, I will," he said, stroking her cheek.

Music filled her head and joy spilled into her heart. She knew he spoke the truth and he'd stop if she asked, but she couldn't say the words to end the bliss that bubbled through her. Instead, she leaned closer and tilted back her head.

"Don't ever stop," she murmured.

Expression grave, he brushed her eyelids gently closed with his thumbs and then kissed them softly, his breath tickling her sensitized skin. While she waited, hardly daring to breathe, he tipped up her chin and settled his lips on hers.

The kiss was so tender, so achingly sweet, that it brought a fresh rush of tears to her eyes. When she attempted to tell him how moved she was, he slipped his tongue inside her mouth.

Quickly, the kiss heated, changed as she clutched at him, seeking to anchor herself so she wouldn't spin away.

"Last chance," he muttered into her hair.

Her answer was to tug his head down and press another kiss to his lips. She didn't realize that he'd opened her shirt until she felt his fingers skate across the sensitive swell of flesh above her bra. When she arched closer, he tore his mouth from hers and buried his face in the hollow between her breasts. Then he stripped away her shirt and bra, leaning back to look down at her in the glow from the lamp.

His expression softened and his lips curved into a smile of approval and wonder. "I knew you'd be beautiful," he whispered, "but I've never seen anyone so exquisite." Slowly, he bent his head and gently suckled one sensitive nipple. Reaction exploded through Kirby as he laved the hardened bud with his tongue. She dug her fingers into his hair, her head thrown back, eyes squeezed shut. He straightened and she slid her hands to his shoulders, pushing off his shirt. Sweet heaven, but he was gorgeously put together.

Pulling off her muddy boots and then his own, he gathered her close and she sighed against his heated skin. When he pushed her gently down, she pulled him with her. He settled his weight along her length, and one of his big hands clasped both her wrists, raised her arms above her head and held them there. She arched her back and his eyes glittered blackly as he feasted on the sight of her breasts.

"Breathtaking," he muttered, then bowed his head and paid homage.

When he had her writhing with need, he freed her wrists. With fingers that trembled, she traced a line from the point of his shoulder to the hollow at the base of his throat and then down the solid plane of his chest to one small brown nub that beaded in anticipation of her touch. When his breath hissed between his teeth, she lifted her head and kissed first one hard nipple and then the other.

His hands tightened in her hair, holding her close. His hips bucked and he turned on the narrow cot, tangling his legs with hers as he ground himself against her. Clutching his waist, she held him close, absorbing his strength and his desire.

He hesitated and her breath caught. If he stopped now, walked out on her again, she'd go mad. Then his hands went to her belt buckle.

"Tell me that you want this."

Her gaze was steady on his. "I want *you.*"

Dusky color splashed across his lean cheeks and his eyes glowed darkly. After he'd stripped them both he wooed her with his hands and his mouth. Only when she begged him, her voice a ragged sob, did he rise over her and take her fully.

Mindless with need, she surrendered to him and to her own passion. Then, when she cried out his name, he slipped the last notch on his own desire and followed her into oblivion.

When Kirby woke up, the room was lighter. The moment she stirred, J.D.'s breathing changed. He turned his head, eyes still shut.

"Good morning." Her smile was tentative.

His reply was a groan, like that of a drunk waking up to a hangover. When he shifted, thick lashes smudgy on his cheeks, and dragged with him the thin blanket they'd found to pull over themselves, cold air assailed her body as doubts assailed her mind.

While she watched, he sat up and slowly opened his eyes. Then he tucked the blanket around her as if he meant to blot out her nakedness. The thin cover was no substitute for his body heat and she shivered.

"Are you okay?" he asked without meeting her gaze.

"Yes. Are you?" She wondered if she appeared as rumpled as she felt, hair a tangle, teeth fuzzy, throat parched. He, on the other hand, looked like a god, all bronzed rippling muscles in the soft morning light, hair miraculously straight, profile a flawless example of classic male beauty.

No doubt his breath was even sweet, she thought wryly. Unlike her own, which felt as sour as the inside of an old boot. Talk about a perfect morning after, bad breath, a partner who wouldn't look her in the eye and no coffee in sight.

Damn. She was about to ask if he was as appalled by their situation as he appeared to be, when he jackknifed from the bed, exposing a fantastic set of male buns, and shrugged into his jeans without bothering with the underwear she distinctly remembered him peeling off the night before.

While she watched from her nest beneath the scratchy blanket, he yanked on socks, boots and shirt.

"I'll go out and give you some privacy," he said, his voice distant. "Then we'd better head back to the truck. I spotted a shovel outside, so I should be able to dig us out. The rain stopped a couple of hours ago."

She hadn't noticed, too drugged from their lovemaking. Had he slept at all? She was tempted to ask if he planned to ignore what had happened between them, but lost her nerve in the face of his closed expression.

"How's your hip?" she asked instead.

He looked surprised. "It's fine."

She ducked her head and began pleating the blanket between her fingers. After a moment of awkward silence, J.D. finally shrugged into his coat and went outside, banging the door shut behind him. As soon as she heard his footsteps fade, Kirby tossed aside the blanket and raced to the tiny bathroom.

Eventually, J.D. ran out of excuses to linger outside. He went back in to find Kirby sitting primly in a chair, fully dressed and hair neatly braided, with her hands folded in her lap. Without his permission, his gaze strayed to the cot. It hadn't seemed so narrow last night.

Images and memories ripped through him, heating his blood. Her response when he'd kissed her—the way she'd arched into him when he suckled her breasts, her nails digging into his scalp—had shredded his control. He'd buried himself deep within her tight body, her muscles caressing him intimately until he exploded while she held him, her tiny cries of pleasure echoing in his head as he poured himself into her.

Now he looked at her bowed head and wondered if he would go mad if he never had her again.

"Are you ready to go?" he asked, his voice as rusty as an old gate.

She raised her head, her green eyes boring through him like lasers. Was it regret he saw there or hurt at the way he'd acted this morning, shutting her out? Had she wanted him to cuddle and caress her? Did she even begin to understand that he couldn't have touched her without taking her again?

The questions continued to plague him as he stared into her eyes, the pupils expanded so the irises were only thin bands of green. Wordlessly, he searched for some clue to her feelings.

"Well," she said briskly, getting to her feet before he could work up the nerve to ask, "I guess there's nothing to keep us here, and I'm sure Donovan is worried sick. I picked a heck of a day to forget the cellular phone.''

J.D. didn't bother to respond, and he had little to say when they were back in the truck and heading home. If she had thought sleeping with him would turn him into a chatterbox, she was doomed to disappointment, she thought dryly as they passed the shack where they'd spent the night. In the daylight, it looked much shabbier than it had in the dark.

J.D. glanced at it when they drove by and a muscle flexed in his cheek. She wondered what he was thinking, and what he'd say if she asked. Her stomach grumbled hollowly, reminding her that she'd missed breakfast, and she pressed a hand over it in a vain attempt to stifle the complaint.

''Will someone else have taken care of the horses?'' she asked when the silence began wearing on her nerves.

''They'd better have.'' He didn't elaborate or even glance at her, so she looked out the passenger window until they finally turned down her brother's driveway. It was probably a futile hope that they'd gotten back early enough for her to slip inside without any fuss. All she wanted was a cup of coffee and a shower before she had to deal with explanations.

When they drove past the main house, she saw Donovan and several of the ranch hands standing by their trucks. When her brother saw them, he gave a shout of relief and hurried over to pull open her door.

''Are you okay?'' he demanded as she went into his arms.

''We're fine,'' she replied, embarrassed at the way the other men were staring. She must look a fright.

She heard J.D.'s door shut and then he walked

around the front of the truck. His expression was forbidding and she knew he must hate being the center of attention even more than she did.

"It's my fault," he told her brother. "I got the truck stuck in mud on a little side road about fifteen miles south of here off Route 6. We spent the night in a deserted cabin and dug the wheels out this morning."

Donovan glanced from J.D. to Kirby. "I found your phone in your Bronco and I was hoping you just got stranded somewhere." He glanced at the knot of interested ranch hands. "Okay, boys. It looks as if we can all get back to work."

When they'd gotten into the other trucks and headed in the direction of the bunkhouse, he turned to J.D. "Thanks for taking care of her."

J.D. nodded. He glanced at Kirby, poker-faced. "See you later."

"Thanks for everything," she said, perversely satisfied when dark color ran up his cheeks.

His eyes narrowed. "No problem." As he circled the truck and slid in behind the wheel, she grabbed her medical bag from the seat and shut the passenger door.

"Kirby! Are you okay?" Bobbie demanded as she burst out of the house. "We've been so worried."

"I'm fine." She looked over her shoulder, but J.D. was already driving away.

"Come on," Bobbie told her, slipping an arm around her waist. "You probably need food and rest. You can tell me all about it while I fix you something in the kitchen."

"I'm fine, really," Kirby insisted as Donovan continued to study her across the dinner table. My God, had she changed so much over one night? Could he somehow tell just by looking at her that she'd been in bed with his horse trainer?

"Thank goodness you weren't alone out there," Bobbie said, dishing peas onto Rose's plate. If she had wondered what Kirby left out of her explanation that morning, she'd been too polite to ask.

It had been difficult for Kirby not to pour out her confused feelings to a sympathetic ear, but she hadn't been ready to confide in anyone. It was J.D. she longed to talk to, and knew she couldn't. He'd erected a wall around himself and she had no idea how to break it down.

"Were you scared?" Rose asked. She'd been told the basics before school, while Kirby was sleeping.

"A little," Kirby admitted.

"But J.D. protected you, didn't he?" Rose seemed to be fascinated that they'd gotten stuck together.

"That's enough, honey," Bobbie cautioned. "We're all glad Aunt Kirby and J.D. are safe. Now let her eat her supper."

"I don't mind," Kirby said. At least Rose's questions were innocent. Kirby would give a lot to know what the other adults on the ranch were thinking. "There wasn't much for him to protect me from," she told Rose. "Mostly, we had to wait for daylight so we could dig the truck out of the mud. Not very exciting, I'm afraid."

Wondering how many black marks she was accumulating for telling little white lies, she looked up from her roast beef and her thoughts to see her brother waiting expectantly.

"I'm sorry, did you say something?" she had to ask. "I guess I'm still a little tired."

"I hope that now you'll consider giving your notice," he replied as he buttered a homemade roll. "Or at least take a leave until the weather's better."

Since he hadn't demanded she quit, Kirby made an effort not to snap back at him. "Why?" she asked instead. "I already told you that if I'd had better directions, we wouldn't have gotten lost. If it hadn't been for the storm, we wouldn't have gotten stuck, and if it hadn't been for J.D.'s hip, we would have walked out to the main road last night." She took a deep, calming breath. "And if I hadn't forgotten the phone in the Bronco, you wouldn't have had to worry. I'm sorry."

"I talked to Reese," Donovan said, laying his knife on the edge of his plate and examining the roll as if he were looking for metal shavings.

Kirby tensed up. Surely J.D. wouldn't have said anything.

"He blames himself for not handling things better."

"He was *wonderful*," Kirby said hotly.

Donovan's brows shot up and even Bobbie appeared to be startled by her vehemence.

"I mean, he was very resourceful," Kirby corrected herself. "He built a fire and he found the shovel to dig out the pickup."

Her brother's shoulders relaxed and he bit into the roll. "He thinks it's his fault you got lost in the first place," he said around the mouthful. "That he should have realized sooner you were on the wrong road."

Kirby started to slide back her chair. "Well, I guess I'll just have to set him straight," she said.

"Why don't you finish your dinner first?" Bobbie suggested. "After the adventure you had, you need the nourishment."

Kirby gazed down at her plate without really seeing it. "Oh, sure," she said absently, but her thoughts were on J.D. What else did he blame himself for besides getting them lost?

Usually the planning of a new project was enough to drive everything else from J.D.'s mind, but tonight his thoughts refused to stay on the rocking chair he was designing. Instead, like silvery minnows darting through the water and then disappearing, they kept returning to Kirby and the night the two of them had spent in each other's arms.

Damn. How stupid could he have been?

He'd tried hard not to need anyone since his grandfather had passed on and his mother got so sick. No one else had ever believed he'd amount to anything. Even his own father hadn't been interested enough to stick around.

The only thing J.D. had ever excelled at, he'd lost. Watching Rose grow, hearing her laugh and seeing her smile, he couldn't regret the way things had gone—not for a minute. And he sure as hell wasn't going to spend the rest of his life whining about bad breaks. Despite Buchanan's assumption to the contrary, J.D. hadn't been playing the hero. His action had been pure reflex. How could he claim credit for something he hadn't even thought about?

Gritting his teeth, he studied the grain of the wood he'd selected. What did Kirby want? he asked himself over and over. How did she see him? As a broken-down ranch hand? As a former rodeo champ? As a man with needs he tried hard to keep under tight control, a man her brother felt obliged to repay?

The questions made him wonder how the hell he really saw himself. He despised self-pity, even though he'd been guilty of wallowing in it for a time while his hip mended.

He picked up a tape measure, but then his hand stilled. Would he ever find some other level of success in his life or had that slipped away with his ability to sit a bull?

When he'd come into his house to change clothes that morning there'd been a message on his answering machine from the woman who ran the gift shop in Sterling, reminding him that he'd promised her more carved boxes. He was astounded that the first ones she'd taken on consignment had sold so quickly. Now she wanted to buy more outright.

"I wish I had the room for larger pieces, too," she'd said, "and the clientele to pay what you're really worth."

He'd played that message over three times. Now he had the urge to tell Kirby about it. Instead, he found a carton and packed up the boxes he'd found the time to finish. The next time Mrs. Buchanan went into Sterling, he knew she'd drop them off for him.

As soon as J.D. had the order ready, he picked up a piece of close-grained applewood he'd been saving for a special project. He studied it for a moment, almost absently, and then he began to carve.

He was still at it when he heard a knock on the door downstairs. Straightening, he rolled his cramped shoulders and glanced at the clock. Then he looked down at the figure in his hand and grimaced. Try as he might to keep his thoughts in line, it was easy to see in which direction his subconscious was leading him.

The knock at the door sounded again and he realized he hadn't heard Snake barking. Perhaps the dog was out on an evening ramble, although he usually waited until later to disappear. When the mutt was in his lair under the front porch, no one got past him, as Kirby had found out the night she'd first learned about her parents' death.

As he went down the stairs, J.D. wondered how she was doing with that whole situation. He'd have liked to bring it up with her, but the habit of not asking personal questions was so deeply ingrained that he found it difficult to break.

Now he wrenched open the door, expecting to find a cowboy in need of some piece of gear for the morning, and instead came face-to-face with the very person who'd been the center of his thoughts and the target of all his lustful longings.

Kirby.

As soon as the front door opened, she began wishing she'd overcome the urge to come down here. J.D. stood with his hand on the knob, surprise stamped on his dark features as he waited for her to state her business.

"I just wanted to make sure you were okay," she said, her breath puffing into the cold air as she resisted the temptation to twist her gloved hands together like a naughty child.

"I'm fine." His tone was blunt, his expression downright forbidding.

As she looked everywhere but at his face, she noticed the fine wood shavings sprinkled on his dark shirt. "I interrupted your work," she said, dismayed. "I'm sorry."

To her surprise, he opened the door wider. "It's okay. I need a break. Want some coffee?"

She couldn't have been more startled if he'd invited her in for a quick tumble. Perhaps that's what he was doing and she was just too naive to recognize it.

He shifted impatiently and she realized she hadn't answered. "Sure," she said quickly. "That sounds good."

She trouped past him and he shut the door behind her. When she hesitated, he reached up to help her out of her jacket. After he'd hung it on a wooden coat tree, he led the way to the kitchen. "I'll make some fresh."

"I didn't mean to put you out." She followed him and sat down in the chair he indicated. The kitchen table was bare except for plain brown salt and pepper shakers, a green paper napkin holder and a bottle of pills. Aspirin, she noticed. "When I didn't see you at the stable, I—"

He glanced around. "You what?" he asked.

"I wondered if your hip was bothering you."

It was the wrong thing to say. She should have known better than to mention his limitation, she realized. Now he'd throw her out for sure.

Instead, he merely turned his back and began to fill the coffeepot with water. "My hip's okay."

She sat quietly while he measured coffee into the filter and plugged in the unit.

"Black, right?" he asked without turning.

"Black's fine." Her gaze wandered over his back, so wide and powerful above a tapered waist, belted with a wide strip of leather, and those compact buttocks covered in denim. Without conscious thought, she remembered how the sight of them naked had stolen her breath.

He turned and saw her watching him, and his brows arched in question. Her cheeks grew hot and her gaze darted around the neat, bare kitchen like a trapped butterfly.

"Snake didn't growl at me," she blurted, desperate for something to say.

"He must not have been here. Sometimes he goes out at night. To hunt, I suppose."

"No," she said, "I saw him. I mean, I saw that one gold eye of his in the glow from my flashlight, but he didn't make a sound."

J.D. was clearly skeptical. "No one gets past him."

Kirby shrugged. She knew what she'd seen. The dog had stared at her, but that was all. She hadn't been entirely sure he wouldn't lunge silently and tear out her throat, but she'd hurried up the steps despite her fear. "*I* got past him," she stated.

J.D. merely shrugged. Then, as if he entertained all the time, he set some cookies she recognized as Bobbie's on a thick white plate and placed it on the table. He leaned against the counter and they waited silently for the coffee to finish brewing, its rich aroma filling the little kitchen.

"Why did you decide to become a nurse?" he asked.

His question surprised and pleased her. "When I was in the fourth grade a little boy cut his arm badly. He might have died if the school nurse hadn't been there to stop the bleeding. I wanted to be able to do things like that. Once I decided on nursing, nothing else ever interested me."

"I remember the way you were with Anna Szabo," he replied. "You care about people."

She flushed with pleasure. "I try to."

"Did your brother tell you this was the original ranch house?" he asked before she could voice one of the many questions she had about him. "They lived here while they built the new place."

"I didn't know that." She glanced around the kitchen with fresh interest, trying to picture Bobbie cooking here.

"Do you want to see the rest of it?"

His offer surprised her. Everything he'd done since she showed up unannounced on his doorstep surprised her. Had sleeping together broken down some of the barriers between them, after all, or was he always this hospitable to women he'd made love to?

Quickly, he showed her the living room, and then he led the way upstairs. Kirby wondered if he was taking her to his bedroom and she was tempted to ask if she could bring her coffee. Then he opened a door and she looked past him, realizing it was his workshop he was showing her. Fascinated, she stepped slowly into the room.

The first thing she noticed was how neat it was, and how pleasant the aroma of raw lumber.

"This is where you made Donovan's door," she murmured as she looked at the stack of wood along one wall, some pieces dark and others as pale as honey. There were books on a shelf and hand tools arranged precisely over a long workbench. She could almost feel the energy in the room.

"I haven't spent as much time here lately as I used to." He went to the window, hands shoved into his pockets, and stared into the night.

"Because you've had to drive me around," she guessed. "If you'd rather, I could ask Donnie if someone else would do it." She held her breath as she stared at his back.

"I can spare the time," he said, turning away from the window. Glancing at the floor, he bent to pick up a wood chip and tossed it into a plastic barrel. Then he faced her again, a muscle flexing in his cheek. "A couple of the men have had their brains stomped on by broncs one too many times. I'd worry if one of them was looking after you."

Kirby was too pleased by his admission to object to the idea that she needed looking after. From his expression, she had an idea that he hadn't meant to say what he had. "I'm glad you feel that way," she replied. The tension between them was suddenly palpable.

In an attempt to diffuse it, she tore her gaze from his. It meant a great deal to her that he'd brought her up here, but she didn't know if she should say anything more. He looked ready to bolt as it was.

Sitting on the workbench was a small, partially finished bust of a woman with long hair. Intrigued, she bent to examine it more closely. She was about to comment on how pretty it was when she recognized the hairstyle and the face.

The small statue was of her.

Chapter Nine

When Kirby looked up from the figure she'd been studying, J.D. was watching her as intently as his dog had.

"Yeah, the carving is you," he admitted, hands jammed into his pockets and shoulders hunched. "I guess we've been spending too much time together. I can't get you out of my head." Clearly, he wasn't happy with the situation.

"I've been thinking about you, too. May I?"

He nodded tersely and she picked up the statue with care, not sure how to take his admission. He sounded as if she were a germ he'd been trying to shake.

"You're very talented." He'd certainly captured her likeness, from her habit of tilting her head, right down to her braid with the hair working loose around her neck.

J.D. came over and took the piece of fine-grained, wheat-colored wood from her. "It doesn't do you justice," he said gruffly. "I'm not done with it yet, but you can have it when I am, if you want."

She debated whether she should accept it or not. She already had the little bird he'd carved. "You'll never get rich if you give all your work away," she said lightly.

"It's a hobby, that's all." He set the bust back down on the bench, stroking one long finger over the top of its head. Kirby remembered the way those fingers had felt on her skin and had to suppress a tremor of longing.

"It could be a lot more than a hobby," she insisted. "Bobbie told me that some of your things have been selling well at a local shop." She traced the abstract design that reminded her of birds in flight that he had carved into the top of a small box. The finish felt like satin. When she lifted the lid, she saw that it was lined with cedar. The sharp aroma prickled her nostrils.

"I just packed up some things for Mrs. Buchanan to drop off there." He pointed to a large carton on the floor.

"May I see them?" Without waiting for his reply, Kirby knelt by the box and opened the flaps.

He squatted down beside her, thigh muscles straining against the worn denim of his jeans. "If you like."

When he shifted, his knee bumped her and he pulled quickly away. At least he wasn't indifferent to her.

As he unwrapped each piece—another small chest, a set of wall plaques, a family of turtles and two little benches covered with flowers and vines—Kirby's excitement grew. They were all wonderful. A plan was forming in her head, but she advanced cautiously.

"Have you ever thought of looking for a different outlet?" she asked when he repacked each item in newspaper. "Maybe a gallery?"

"I'm not an artist. I do this to relax." He tucked the last plaque in the carton, stood up and extended a hand to help her.

"You have talent," she argued. "Don't sell yourself short." The warmth of his hand wrapped around hers was distracting, as was the closeness of his rangy body. Had he moved nearer when she stood up? She suddenly felt crowded, her senses coming alive in a totally different way than when she'd first looked into the room and smelled the raw wood.

"I want you to have the statue," he said without releasing her fingers, "but forget about trying to turn me into something I'm not."

Before she could protest, he caught the back of her head with his free hand and covered her mouth with his. Reaction exploded along her nerve endings and she clutched at him as she swayed.

The moment J.D.'s lips touched hers, he knew this wild, sweet sensation that knocked him sideways whenever he was close to her was what had driven him to carve the bust. His mouth moved over hers as he savored her taste. He dragged her scent into his lungs, senses swimming.

When she gripped the front of his shirt and tipped back her head to accommodate his exploration of her jaw and throat, exultation slammed into him. His body responded with a surge of pure greed. He wanted her, all of her. With a ragged groan, he bent and scooped her into his arms, heading for his bedroom as she murmured his name.

Before he could tumble her to the bed, the phone on the nightstand began ringing. Kirby's arms tightened around his neck.

"Don't answer it," she whispered into his ear.

"I have to. It could be your brother." Buchanan knew J.D. would be here if he wasn't at the stable. The last thing he wanted was for the man to show up on his porch. Swearing under his breath, J.D. set her on her feet, switched on the lamp and reached for the receiver.

Kirby watched his lean face and hooded eyes while he snarled a greeting into the phone and then listened, expression unreadable. Had he been as disappointed by the interruption as she was? She'd wanted to be swept away by passion without a chance to think about why she had actually come here. Now she had to deal with reality, knowing she'd sought him out because she couldn't stay away, couldn't wonder for another moment if last night had meant anything more to him than an opportunity that had been dumped in his lap by circumstance.

She'd hated the way he'd acted this morning. After he'd withdrawn behind his wall of silence back at the shack, what other choice had there been for her except to retreat as well?

Now that she'd had time to think, though, she wanted to explore this edgy attraction between them, to see where the passion they'd found in each other's arms might lead. And she wanted to know how he felt, what he was thinking behind those black eyes that were so difficult to read.

After J.D. had listened to the voice on the other

end of the line for several moments, he gave the caller a couple of brief orders, something about a horse that had pulled up lame.

"If I get there and he's picked up a rock or has a loose shoe, I'm not going to be happy," J.D. warned. "Yeah, okay. I'll see you in a few minutes."

At his parting words, disappointment streaked through her. "Emergency?" she asked when he broke the connection. She was hugging herself with her arms in an attempt to keep from reaching for him.

"You think I'm looking for a reason to go back out there tonight?" he demanded, frowning. His gaze wandered down her body and back again, lingering on her breasts until they tingled. "I'd rather stay here." He didn't add, "with you," but his voice was husky with promise.

"I could go with you," she suggested.

He shook his head. "I don't want to expose you to any more speculation after last night. Randy has a big imagination and a bigger mouth."

"Why do you have to go?" she asked. Maybe he would come right back.

"His horse pulled up lame this afternoon and now he wants me to check it out. I wish to hell he'd called earlier."

"I could wait for you here."

"I don't know how long I'll be."

Didn't he want her? Didn't he trust her in his house? Desperation seized her. "If it gets too late, I'll just leave."

Shaking his head, he shackled her wrist with his fingers and led her from the bedroom. "You need to go back to the house before your brother comes look-

ing for you,'' he told her as he started down the stairs
with her still in tow.

Kirby wasn't about to suggest that she call Donovan and tell him not to worry. She was a big girl, but
she could see that J.D. had lost interest. Then why
had he kissed her, taken her into his bedroom? Why
had he insisted she have the statue?

Now wasn't the time to ask. ''Don't let me hold
you up,'' she said instead, her voice stiff with hurt.

At the base of the stairs he glanced around sharply.
Standing on the step, she was almost level with him.
He let go of her wrist, grabbed her shoulders and
tugged, so she fell against him. Holding her chin, he
kissed her firmly. When she reached for him, though,
he stepped back.

''Part of my job's looking out for the horses,'' he
said, his gaze riveted on her mouth. ''That's why your
brother keeps me around. That and his guilty conscience.''

His bitter words startled her. Is that what J.D.
thought? Donovan had told her he was a gifted
trainer. Perhaps she could speak to her brother.

''City girl, I have to go,'' J.D. added, grabbing her
jacket off the coat tree when she merely looked at
him. ''And you have to go back to the main house.''

If he would only tell her he wanted to stay, instead
of acting so impatient.

''Thank you so much for the lovely statue,'' she
remembered to say as he held up her jacket. ''And
please give some thought to what I said about your
carvings. You could do a lot better than a little gift
shop in Sterling.''

His frown deepened as he shrugged into his own
jacket and grabbed his Stetson. ''I know what I am.

If you don't like the idea of going to bed with a ranch hand, there are probably other men around here who'd be happy to accommodate you.'' Shoulders rigid, he stalked to the door while she gaped after him.

Her hand itched to smack him. "I didn't mean..." she began instead.

Holding open the door, he watched her with an unreadable expression while the cold air poured over her. "I know just what you're trying to do. And I'm out of time. If you don't want a man to get the wrong impression, don't show up at his place uninvited.''

"Don't worry, I won't make the same mistake again.'' Heat climbed Kirby's cheeks at the unfairness of his words. Furious, she stuck out her chin and sailed past him through the open door. If he wanted to be so pigheaded, she'd be damned if she'd try to dissuade him.

Her anger carried her halfway back to the main house before she first became aware of a noise behind her. Whirling around, she recognized the single gold eye of J.D.'s dog, Snake, shining in the darkness. He was following her.

"What do you want?'' she demanded, too upset to be afraid. "Your master has already chewed me up tonight.'' Just let the damned dog try to bite her and she'd club him with her flashlight.

Silently, Snake tipped his head, never blinking or taking his one good eye off her as he sat down in the road. Now that she could see him, he appeared to be part Husky or German Shepherd, with coarse black-and-gray fur and a sharp, intelligent face. One of his ears was missing the tip, as if it had been bitten off, and she wondered how he'd lost his other eye.

"Oh, I suppose you're just escorting me home?" she guessed with the beginning of a smile. He'd been there under the porch tonight, even while J.D. was insisting she couldn't have gotten past the dog without making him bark. Wait until she told him ol' Snake had walked her back to the house.

Hand extended, Kirby advanced on him slowly, talking nonsense in a low, steady voice. It was the same method she'd seen J.D. use on horses.

When Snake laid back his ears and lifted his lip to expose shiny teeth, she assumed he didn't want her to touch him. For now, it was enough that he didn't growl.

"Okay," she said, dropping her hand and stepping back, "if you aren't ready, I'm sure as heck not going to push it."

Muttering under her breath about strays and loners, she walked on up to the house. The porch light was on as always, so she snapped off the beam of her flashlight. When she turned to tell Snake he could go, the road that unfurled into the darkness was empty. For a moment, she searched for some sign of the dog, but there was none. Shaking her head and wondering if she could possibly have imagined his presence, she went into the house.

Kirby had the next day off, and there was also a teachers' workshop day at school. It had snowed in the night, but the sky had cleared that morning and now bare spots were beginning to appear on the road. A friend of Bobbie's was coming to lunch and bringing her two children along to play with Rose.

"You're welcome to stay," Bobbie insisted when Kirby told her she was going to Taylor's. "I know you and Renee would like each other and her kids are nice enough.''

"Thanks, hon, but I've been meaning to take Ashley up on her invitation and I want to see the boys again. She promised that Taylor would come back for lunch if I went over, so it's a good time for me to see them all.''

Kirby felt a little guilty; she'd been so preoccupied with her feelings about J.D. that she'd neglected her own family, and they were the reason she'd elected to extend her stay.

"Tell them hi for me,'' Bobbie said.

When Kirby left a little while later, she thought she caught a glimpse of J.D. walking down the road from the stable toward the bunkhouse, but she couldn't be sure. The whole time she was at Taylor's, it was hard not to let him slip into her thoughts.

"Is there something on your mind?'' her older brother demanded as soon as lunch was over and the two of them had settled down with their coffee. Ashley had refused Kirby's offer to help clean up after an excellent meal of French dip sandwiches from their own beef and homemade fries. Instead, she'd shooed Bobbie and Taylor out of the room and sent the boys outside to play while she tackled the dishes.

There was something about his quiet demeanor as well as his reassuring bulk that invited confidences, Kirby thought as she blew on her hot coffee. She knew that Donovan loved her and looked out for her, sometimes more than she wanted. Taylor, however, was a rock she could count on, there if she needed him. She'd seen him only a few times, but she'd talked to him on the phone nearly every evening since her arrival.

Now he sat patiently, one long leg crossed over the other, and stirred cream into his mug as if they had all the time in the world. She knew his days were usually spent working outdoors with his men; Ashley had confided when Kirby arrived that she was glad to have him around the house for a few hours instead.

"How well do you know J.D. Reese?" she asked him, breaking a piece off a freshly baked molasses cookie and popping it into her mouth.

Taylor took a moment to answer. When she finally looked up, his dark eyes were twinkling. "Is that the way of it?" He pursed his lips thoughtfully. "I wondered what's been on your mind besides family."

"He hasn't been on my mind," she denied swiftly.

His dark, straight brows arched and his mouth quirked. "No? You only want to know about him in his capacity of horse trainer?"

"Well," she amended after she'd nibbled at the cookie, "I guess that's not quite true. He's...an interesting man. I suppose Donovan told you we got stranded together during that last storm?"

Taylor reached for a cookie but didn't bite into it. "He mentioned it. Said Reese took good care of you. Anything else I should know about that night?"

She shook her head. She wasn't about to supply details, since she didn't want either brother going after J.D. with a shotgun.

"The Bronco wasn't running," she said, "and the cellular phone was in it, so we had to wait for daylight in order to dig our way out of the mud, that's all." She hoped her heated cheeks didn't betray her.

Apparently, Taylor saw nothing amiss, or chose not to. "Reese is a good man," he said after he'd disposed of the cookie in two bites and washed it down with a mouthful of coffee. "He was handed a bad break for doing the right thing, and it's scarred him, I think. I don't know much about his background. He always stayed to himself when I was on the circuit. If he hung around with anyone, it was some of the Indian bronc riders. He had a real gift for the bulls, though, a natural seat, and he was the only man in the running I thought had a chance to beat Donnie at the Nationals."

"That's what he told me," Kirby replied.

"J.D. did?"

"No, Donovan. He told me about the accident. That's how J.D. ended up at the ranch."

"That's right," Taylor agreed. "Donnie went down to the Navajo reservation twice before he managed to drag him back here. J.D.'s a proud man, not easy with accepting help. There are simpler roads, if you're looking for someone special."

"My head knows that," Kirby confessed, "but it doesn't seem to matter."

"The heart chooses its own path," Taylor said, charming her. Her elder brother was a complex man and Ashley was a lucky woman to have him. "Be careful, though. A man like J.D. could be as unbending as an iron bar. Right or wrong, he may have too much pride to ever come to a woman empty-handed."

Kirby wondered if that had been something Taylor had had to overcome as well. He hadn't always had the ranch; she knew that he and Donnie had rodeoed for years before they each became successful.

"Have you seen J.D.'s woodworking?" she asked. "I'm sure you know that he was the one who did Donnie's front door. He's very talented."

Taylor uncrossed his booted feet. "I've asked J.D.

to do a chest for Ashley, but he refuses to name a price and I won't accept something like that without paying him. So far, we're at a standoff. He'd have a second career if he wasn't so prickly about taking a helping hand once in a while. He walks a solitary path.''

Taylor eyed Kirby with a tolerant expression. ''At least he has until now.''

His words confirmed something she'd been considering. Briefly, she outlined her idea.

He shook his head slowly. ''You'd have to be careful how you went about this scheme,'' he warned. ''One hint that you were behind it and he'd probably balk. I told you he's proud.''

''Pigheaded is more like it, but there are ways around that, I'm sure.'' What J.D. didn't know couldn't possibly hurt him, and she was sure her brother Jonathan would be more than happy to cooperate with her. Suddenly she was eager to get back home and call him.

Draining her coffee mug, she gave Taylor a big smile. ''Thanks for your input, but now I'm sure I've taken you away from work long enough.''

She got to her feet and began picking up their dishes while he watched her with his usual serious expression. Then he stood, too.

''Don't rush off,'' he said.

''I want to get back. I'll just pop back in the kitchen to thank Ashley for lunch and then I'll be going.''

''In that case, I think I'll check on the boys and maybe see if my wife wants to take a little nap.'' Taylor's dark eyes were gleaming and his mouth had softened into a grin. Before Kirby could take the dishes to the kitchen, he tipped up her chin with one finger. "Be careful," he warned. "Remember that I'm here if you need anything or want to talk. Have you heard from the Wilsons?"

Kirby shook her head. "When I talked to Jonathan he asked if I'd call them, but I haven't been ready to." She still hadn't reconciled her feelings toward them.

"Remember, they did raise you as their own daughter."

Taylor's comment surprised her. She would have expected him to be more biased. Donovan was firmly in her corner.

"I would rather they'd told me the truth," she said. "They kept denying it even after Donovan confronted them."

"They were afraid," Taylor replied. "I'm not trying to excuse them, just reminding you they were far from all bad."

She remembered Donovan telling her about the old rancher who had taken in her brothers and how the man had provided a roof over their heads with no real affection. She could have had it a lot worse, she realized.

"I know what you're saying is true," she admitted. "I just have to work things out in my own mind. As wonderful as you've all been to me, I'm still sorting through everything."

Taylor nodded. "It's a lot to deal with. Perhaps it's not the best time to rush into anything else," he cautioned.

She knew what he was referring to. "I'm trying to take it slow." She leaned closer and gave him a kiss on the cheek. It was obvious that her gesture pleased him. "Thanks, bro," she murmured. "I'll keep you posted."

"That's all I ask," he replied before he followed her back to the kitchen with a grin she knew had nothing whatever to do with her.

"Martin and I loved the little box you sent," Jonathan told Kirby over the phone. "I just wanted you to know that I'll be contacting Mr. Reese ASAP to see if I can get a peek at more of his work. If it's all as good as I suspect it will be and he's able to do bigger pieces as well, we may be able to offer him an exclusive contract for the gallery."

"Just remember not to say anything about being related to me," Kirby cautioned. She disliked the subterfuge, but after her talk with Taylor she was convinced it was the only way J.D. would cooperate.

Later on, when he'd seen for himself that it was his talent bringing him the success she was convinced he was capable of achieving, she'd tell him the truth. By then he'd understand why it had been necessary for her to keep back a few details.

"I'll remember, hon." Jonathan went on to recite, "I saw a piece that a friend bought at a shop in Sterling."

When he'd questioned the secrecy, she'd merely told him J.D. was determined to make it on his own.

"I even called the owner, a nice woman named Kent, so the story would check out if he happened to talk to her," Jon added. "Now that you've whetted our appetites, I hope our boy has got the time to do some things we can really showcase."

J.D. had several horses to get ready for a sale in Denver, so he didn't see Kirby for nearly a week. As busy as he was, the hours spent away from her dragged slowly. Even the sale itself failed to bring him the deep feeling of accomplishment he usually experienced every time Buchanan stock brought top dollar.

"Couldn't have done it without you," Kirby's brother told him after they'd loaded up the two fillies the buyer from Nebraska had arranged to pick up later in the month. "We got good money for every horse we sold." He pumped J.D.'s hand enthusiastically. "Why don't you let me buy you some dinner? I'm heading back later tonight and I can give you a lift if there's anything you want to stick around here for."

Perhaps he should have accepted the offer. J.D. had a feeling, though, that Donovan wanted to quiz him a little more about the night he'd spent with Kirby, and that was the last thing he felt like discussing— with anyone.

He hadn't yet been able to sort out his feelings for her. Except that he wanted her with an ache that damn near doubled him over, and crawling into his bed alone at night had gotten one hell of a lot tougher than it used to be.

He didn't want to hang around Denver any longer than necessary. He was in a hurry to get back to the ranch and check on Popcorn, the filly he was buying from Buchanan.

"Thanks, but I'll just grab a ride with Charlie," he replied with a nod in the direction of the ranch pickup. J.D.'s one consolation in being away was that Charlie Babcock had come to the sale with them, leaving an older wrangler to drive Kirby to see her patients when the weather turned threatening. She'd been learning her way around and most days she went by herself.

Buchanan's grin faltered only slightly, making J.D. feel bad about turning him down. He wasn't a difficult man to work for. The other hands all liked him, joking and talking with him as if he were one of them instead of the boss. Only J.D. kept to his usual practice of not mixing with any of them, but he wondered what it would be like to feel the same easy familiarity with the others he'd witnessed at the bunkhouse or on the job.

"I want to do a little shopping for Bobbie and Rose," Buchanan said with a wink. "So I guess I'll see you back at the spread."

J.D. hooked a thumb through his belt. "Charlie said something about grabbing a burger on the way out of town." He glanced at the gleaming black horse trailer that had been full when they'd arrived. It was going back empty except for the two fillies.

Buchanan raised a hand to Charlie, who sat behind the wheel chewing gum. "Safe trip," he told J.D., and then he walked away.

By the time Charlie and J.D. had driven back to the Rocking Rose, unloaded the horses and taken care of the chores, the only things on J.D.'s mind were coffee and bed. He didn't even give a damn that the latter would be empty, as usual.

When he finally walked past Snake into his house, shoulders drooping with fatigue, and headed to the kitchen with the dog's empty dish, he was surprised to see the light blinking on his answering machine.

He'd bought the machine at a thrift store on a whim, but the only person who ever left messages was the woman from the gift shop, nagging him for more pieces. He assumed this message was to acknowledge the carton he'd sent. Or perhaps she'd decided his stuff wasn't good enough to sell, after all.

He waited until the coffee was perking and the dog was fed before he bothered to turn on the machine. He listened once and then he played it back a second time before the message sank in.

Someone from Aspen wanted to talk to him about his carving. They might be interested in featuring his work at their furniture gallery. J.D. sat at the kitchen table and sipped his coffee as he listened to the message for a third time.

Even when he'd seen fancy ads in glossy cowboy magazines for everything from designer Western wear to art made from barbed wire and wrought iron, he'd never thought of his own work as anything more than a hobby. Now this voice on the machine was telling him he had talent and showed real promise.

J.D. had been tempted to laugh until the caller mentioned the price he'd have charged for the small jewelry box—three times what it sold for in Sterling. A little fast figuring had wiped the grin from J.D.'s face like chalk off a slate.

That kind of money would buy tools for future projects—and choice wood to make them. Perhaps he'd give this character a call back tomorrow, just to hear what the man had to say.

Until then, there was no cause to get excited. And no reason to imagine Kirby's reaction to his news, but he spent most of the night dreaming up scenarios just the same.

Kirby had seen J.D. only once since he'd gotten back from the sale in Denver, and they hadn't been alone. This morning she hadn't expected to run into him at all. She had only two nursing assignments and they were both easy to find, so she was driving herself.

She was headed for the Bronco, medical bag in hand, when J.D. came riding down the road on Buck. The picture the two of them made was such an attractive one she had to stand and watch with a silly smile on her face until he'd pulled up beside her.

"Good morning, cowboy," she said breathlessly as Buck shook his head and blew noisily from his flared nostrils.

"I'm glad I caught you," he replied. "You're on your way early this morning."

"I have a meeting in town before my appointments," she admitted. As usual, he was so attractive that her heart spun in her chest.

"Would you go to dinner with me tonight?"

Had she heard him right? "You want me to go to dinner with you?" she echoed foolishly. He'd think she'd never been asked out before in her life. She'd never dated anyone for the first time *after* they'd been to bed together, though.

Buck danced impatiently, as if to say he wanted to get going. J.D. controlled him with easy competence, and Kirby thought she saw a glimmer of laughter in his dark eyes. No doubt it was her own total lack of poise he found amusing.

"That's right," he said gravely. "I realize it's late notice and that you may have other plans, but—"

"I'd love to," she said before he could withdraw the invitation. "What time?"

"Pardon me?" Apparently, it was his turn to be surprised.

"What time should I be ready?"

"Is six too early? I've got horses to see to at first light tomorrow."

"Six is fine. How should I dress?" She was dying to ask what had brought about this change in him, but she'd probably find out later.

"Wear whatever you like," he said. "We'll go to Chandler's, if that's okay with you."

She knew from Bobbie that, while not fancy, Chandler's had the best steaks this side of Denver and prices to put a serious dent in a cowpoke's wallet.

"That would be nice. I haven't been there yet. Are we celebrating something?" she asked. Perhaps Donovan had given him a bonus after the horse sale.

Removing his Stetson with a sweep of his hand, J.D. leaned down and planted a kiss on her upturned mouth. "You bet we are," he said with uncharacteristic enthusiasm. "I'll explain when I see you."

While Kirby stared, bemused, he whirled Buck around and galloped back down the road. She was just getting into the Bronco, shaking her head in disbelief, when she heard what sounded like a war cry. Looking up, she saw Buck rear up on his back legs. J.D. waved his hat and then the two of them disappeared from sight behind the stable.

"What was that all about?" Bobbie asked, coming out the back door. "If I didn't know better, I'd swear that rider was J.D. Reese."

"It was," Kirby replied, relieved to know that she hadn't imagined the whole thing. "I think we just made a date for dinner."

Chapter Ten

"He's late." Kirby's voice was flat, the disappointment pooling in her stomach bitter and cold as she started to get up from the kitchen table. J.D. had had second thoughts.

"It's only five to six." Bobbie's tone was full of understanding, but her smile was edged with humor as she loaded the dishwasher. "Give the poor man a few more minutes before you write him off."

"Perhaps I should wait for him outside."

"It's frigid out there, and besides, J.D. knows the way to my kitchen," Bobbie replied as she covered a platter of leftover roast beef from the family's supper and put it in the refrigerator. "Got any idea what you're celebrating?"

"I don't have a clue."

Bobbie hadn't expressed much surprise over Kirby's dinner plans, but Donovan had made a few mother-hen noises before she shushed him. Rose had started to ask questions, but Bobbie distracted her, and now Donovan was supervising his daughter's bath.

Kirby toyed nervously with a cup of coffee she didn't want, staring at her reflection in the dark liquid, while Bobbie hummed under her breath and wiped off the tile counter. Jonathan had called earlier to give Kirby a progress report, but there was no way she could tell anyone until J.D. revealed the news himself.

This was a lot more complicated than she'd first envisioned. It had been difficult knowing her brother was in town without being able to see him, but a visit would have been too risky. What if someone spotted them and mentioned it in front of J.D.?

"This has got to be something big," Bobbie said. "Chandler's may not have linen tablecloths and snooty waiters, but the food's great and the prices aren't cheap."

"Do you think I'm making a mistake?" Kirby asked as she poked at the hair she'd worn loose and wavy. She hoped her long, black print skirt and white sweater weren't too dressy; she'd tried on a half-dozen outfits before pairing this one with skinny black boots. A red wool coat she'd borrowed from Bobbie was folded over the back of another chair with her black purse.

"Do *you* think you are?"

Before Kirby could reply, they heard the clump of boots on the deck outside. A knock on the kitchen door had Kirby drawing in a nervous breath as Bobbie wiped her hands on her apron.

"Want me to get that?"

Kirby was already pushing back her chair with

hands that trembled. "No, thanks, I'll do it." Her mouth had gone dry, making speech difficult.

Usually J.D. poked his head in the door after he knocked, but this time he waited for her to turn the knob. When she had, she stared up at him until he shifted self-consciously.

"Am I too early?"

She wouldn't have thought it possible, but he looked even more attractive than usual. He was wearing crisp black jeans and a blue plaid Western shirt under a black denim jacket with a sheepskin collar. It was far from new, but spotlessly clean. His hair was pulled back from his face, emphasizing its strong, spare lines, and he held his hat in one hand.

"You're right on time," Kirby managed to say. "I'm ready." She opened the door wider and stepped aside, but he stayed where he was as he surveyed her from head to foot and back again. She was tempted to execute a pirouette, but managed to restrain herself.

"Very nice." His voice was gravelly and his eyes were hooded.

"You, too," she replied. "Would you like to come in for a minute?"

Wary as any teenage suitor, he stepped past her, his gaze cutting through the kitchen like a mine sweeper. When he saw Bobbie, his shoulders relaxed slightly and he grinned, the corners of his eyes crinkling.

"Wow," she said, returning his smile. "You look fantastic."

He ducked his head, but it was obvious her comment pleased him. Kirby wished she'd been able to say something as spontaneous, instead of worrying how she might sound if she did. Taking a deep breath, she reached for her coat as J.D. did the same. Their hands collided and she snatched hers back as if she'd touched the wrong end of a branding iron.

"I'll get it." Impatience edged his voice. Perhaps he was regretting this date already. He held the coat out and leaned closer as she slid her arms into it. "Mmm, you smell good."

"Too strong?" she asked, jerking away. She loathed it when a woman reeked of perfume.

His expression softened. "Just right."

Kirby was a bundle of nerves, he realized. Beneath all that polish, she wasn't as confident as she wanted him to think. The knowledge gave him a rush, followed by a melting tenderness that had him blinking in surprise.

She shifted beneath his hands and he realized that he was still gripping her shoulders. He forced his gloved fingers to relax at the same moment he noticed Bobbie's thoughtful expression. Did she disapprove? Her gratitude had always ridden easier on him than her husband's did.

And how did *he* feel about this? J.D. couldn't afford to put his job on the line, but a man usually knew where he stood with Buchanan.

The reason for tonight's celebration ricocheted through him. Someday he'd be his own man again, he vowed silently.

"Don't wait up for us," he said aloud. Kirby glanced up at him, a question in her eyes. "Okay with you?" he asked.

Her smile was all the answer he needed, but she nodded as well. He felt like a million bucks and it had nothing to do with the deal he'd signed earlier.

"Do I have to wait till dinner to find out what

we're celebrating?" Kirby demanded as soon as he'd tucked her into his truck beside him and started the engine.

"I don't know if I can wait that long," he admitted, driving down the road to the main highway. Funny, the first person he'd wanted to share the news with had been her. That should have worried him; instead he was just glad she was here beside him now.

"Oh, please don't keep me waiting," she coaxed with a little pout. "Tell me now." She batted her eyes for effect and he grinned.

What he really wanted was to kiss her, he realized with a sharp ache, to possess her again. The thought made his palms sweat, made him throb with excitement and impatience.

First things first, he reminded himself. Dinner, and then they'd see about the other. He glanced in the rearview mirror. Were they far enough from the house to pull over without anyone else noticing? He eased on the brake but left the motor running.

"Are you warm enough?" he asked, to prolong the suspense.

"Yes!" She grabbed the lapels of his jacket. "Quit stalling!"

His control wavered and then shattered like cheap glass. Hauling her close, he kissed her hard. As soon as he felt her mouth soften and melt, molding itself to his, he gentled the kiss. The temptation to turn the truck around and burn rubber all the way back to his house—and the hell with her brother—had him shaking.

Then he thought about how pretty she looked in her sweater and skirt with her hair a honey gold cascade. She deserved a nice dinner before he fell on her like a starving dog. An inch at a time, he made himself release her.

"Are you okay?" Had he hurt her, bruised her tender mouth?

Her voice floated between them. "Mmm? Oh, yes, I'm fine." She didn't sound like a woman who hadn't wanted to be kissed.

Apparently, she'd forgotten all about his news—as he nearly had for a moment himself.

He took a deep breath. "A fellow from Aspen who owns some kind of furniture gallery saw one of the carved boxes Mrs. Kent sold in her shop."

Kirby held her breath, striving for the right degree of curiosity and excitement. The excitement needed no faking. "And?" she prompted.

J.D. looked out the windshield for a moment while she wondered if she'd done the right thing. "And?" she repeated.

He rubbed his jaw with his gloved hand. "He wanted to see more of my stuff, so I met him in town."

Kirby let her breath leak out. "Did he like them?" she asked, feeling her way slowly.

"Yeah." The emotions he packed into that one word—shock, excitement and pride—were easy to identify.

Relief seeped through her. Her instincts had been right; this was going to work. "Will he be buying some things from you?" she asked innocently.

"He offered me an exclusive contract for everything I create from wood, but he's leaving the details up to me."

"That's wonderful." The smile she gave J.D. was the genuine article, the soaring happiness she felt on his behalf as authentic as a new hundred-dollar bill. She leaned over and kissed his cheek. "I knew you had talent."

His grin was crooked. "Thanks, honey. It's still a shock to me that a total stranger would feel the same way."

His words gave her a moment's unease, but his expression was guileless. "I guess we'd better get to town or we'll miss our reservations."

Squeezing the hand that gripped hers, Kirby sat back and recalled Jonathan's comments on the phone. "I can't thank you enough for sending your cowboy to us," he had enthused. "We love what he's doing with wood and we're going to handle everything he can produce. Trust me, he'll be a sensation."

And J.D. would understand why she'd felt the need to go behind his back, she told herself now. Of course he would.

J.D. pulled out on the main road and risked a glance at the woman seated beside him. In the glow from the dash he could see her face, and she looked anxious. Was she having second thoughts about whether he could pull this off?

Jonathan Wilson had called him talented. And promising. J.D. wouldn't get rich—not on what he had time to do—but he'd be paid, and handsomely, if he was to believe Wilson, for something he created with his hands and his instinct.

"Don't worry," he said aloud. "I can do this." Listen to him boasting. How ironic that two of the people who'd encouraged him had the same last name.

"You don't have a cousin in Aspen, do you?" he asked.

"C-cousin?" she stammered. "No, why?"

Briefly, he explained.

"Wilson's a common name."

"True enough." He pressed his foot down on the accelerator. "Tonight we celebrate." He slung his arm around her shoulders and gave her a squeeze.

Kirby aimed at his cheek another kiss that actually bounced off his jaw. His blood bubbled in his veins as he chuckled.

The excitement held him in its grip all through dinner, an excellent meal he didn't even mind forking over a big chunk of his month's salary for.

Seated across from him in the high-backed booth, Kirby plied him with questions, peppered him with compliments, dazzled him with adoring glances. A more cynical man might have wondered how much of this apparent adoration was due to his suddenly more promising future.

J.D. didn't care. If the deal worked out, he might have something more to offer than a tiny house and a dead-end job.

The idea stopped him cold. What was he thinking? That a few pieces of whittling were going to change him, lighten his skin, give him a real chance with a woman like Kirby?

He'd just paid the bill and they were hurrying through the cold to the truck. She slid her hand into his and his heart started to pump. In a little while, if she was willing, he'd have her wrapped around him like a quilt.

That was what he wanted, he reminded himself—the heat, the sizzle, the wild, wonderful loving they'd shared before. Beyond that, he refused to consider.

For tonight at least, her enthusiastic presence in his bed was all he wanted.

Kirby didn't say a word when he drove past the main house without slowing. Perhaps he meant only to walk her back from his place—and perhaps to kiss her good-night without an audience. If he did, she'd resist the temptation to beg him to let her stay. And the urge to put her arms around him and hang on for dear life.

"Snake walked me home the other night," she said as they pulled up in the circle of light spilling from his porch.

"The hell he did." J.D.'s hand stilled on the door handle of his pickup. "If that mutt threatens you, I'll shoot him myself."

"Oh, no," she gasped. "He was the perfect gentleman. I tried to pet him and he didn't even growl."

J.D.'s eyes widened with shock. "You did *what?* I can't believe he didn't take your hand off at the wrist. He won't even let me touch him, and I've been feeding him for months. You're not to go anywhere near him, you understand?"

Kirby leaned away from J.D. on the bench seat. "He wouldn't hurt me," she insisted. "He's just not quite ready to be petted."

J.D. made a strangled noise in his throat and then he snared her hand, clamping hard enough on her gloved fingers to make her wince. "The dog is dangerous."

"Nonsense. But I'll be careful, if it will make you feel better." She tugged on her hand until he freed it. Then she looked past him toward his house. "Going to offer a girl a cup of coffee?" she asked.

His black eyes glinted with interest. "Coffee's the least of what I'm offering." Before she could suck in a breath or brace herself for the attack on her senses, he was kissing her. His hands clenched in her hair, holding her still so he could ravage her mouth. Need surged inside her, blood pounding in her head; she twined her arms around his neck and kissed him back with all the pent-up emotion inside her.

Too soon he broke the kiss and touched his brow to hers. "Come inside with me?"

She almost chuckled that he still phrased it as a question. "Try and stop me."

He all but dragged her from the car, steadying her when her feet hit the ground, then hustled her up the steps and through the door like a man possessed. As soon as he'd shoved it closed, he pressed her up against it, his hips pinning her there as he cupped her jaw with his hands and dived into another kiss.

Reaction whipped through her like the hot wind of a dust devil. Her fingers went to the snaps on his shirt while he pulled at her coat. Bobbie's coat. She rescued it before it hit the floor.

"Sorry," he muttered, tossing it and the jacket he shrugged out of onto the nearby couch. A single light burned there. By the time he'd turned back to her she had her sweater over her head. It followed the coats. His shirt was hanging open, revealing the hard contours of his chest. She was doing her best to step out of her skirt as they made their way up the stairs, his arm around her waist. When the skirt nearly tripped her, she started to giggle softly.

He dropped a kiss onto her hair and the laughter died in her throat. He'd been a surprisingly entertaining companion over dinner. Not talkative; he'd never be that. He was, though, an attentive listener, and he'd drawn her out with questions. Questions about her family in Boise—she'd felt pangs of guilt at leaving out Jonathan's name—and the marriage she'd shrugged off with a brief explanation. Her divorce still felt like a failure.

She'd mentioned thinking about contacting the Wilsons, and J.D. had surprised her by urging her to do so. He commented on the importance of family, and she could see a hint of the loneliness behind his facade of indifference. When she'd asked about his past, he'd actually unbent enough to tell her of his father's desertion and his mother's death. No wonder he wanted her to stay in touch with her adopted parents.

It was only when she'd asked about his bull-riding career that he clammed up. Obviously, the loss was still too painful for him to discuss, so she switched the topic to his carving. With the encouragement of an old rodeo clown and a how-to manual from a thrift store, J.D. had taught himself while he waited his turn behind the chutes of a couple hundred rodeos.

When he and Kirby finally reached the top of the stairs, she in her teddy and boots, he bare-chested with his belt buckle undone, he swooped her into his arms. His scent—after-shave, soap and compelling male—swirled around her as she linked her arms about his neck.

Holding her tightly, he pushed open the door to his bedroom and kicked it shut behind them while she pressed her lips to his shoulder. Then she tilted back her head and studied his face.

The only light in the room was the glow of the moon. In its reflection, his skin was pale and shadowed, his lashes darker smudges on his cheeks and his eyes as unreadable as black glass.

"You deserve flowers and candy." His voice in the silence surprised her. "Fabulous jewels to enhance your beauty."

"I don't need them."

His arms tightened, the muscles flexed. "I should be courting you."

"Tonight was wonderful," she told him, fascinated by the bones and hollows of his face and shape of his mouth as he talked. That sensual, talented, generous mouth. She traced his lower lip with her finger.

"Tonight's not over yet." With that, he opened his arms and dropped her onto the bed. She barely had time to utter a little squawk of protest before he'd followed her down and covered her body with his.

J.D. meant to at least start slow and tender, but his blood had been simmering since he'd walked into the Buchanan kitchen, boiling since the two of them had pulled up outside his house in the truck. He was doing well not to strip Kirby naked and bury himself to the hilt in her tight, wet heat as his body urged him to. Before he'd met her, he would have prided himself on his finesse, his control, but she stripped them from him like varnish off old wood, leaving him bare, hungry and trembling with need.

Gathering her to him, he rolled so she was above him. Her golden hair hung around her face like a halo, but she looked far from angelic as she bent to attack him with her lips and tongue.

Her mouth closed over one sensitive male nipple as her busy fingers caressed the other. His vision fogged, then cleared enough for him to see her lids sweep down over her eyes as she threw back her head.

Again they shifted, legs tangled, bodies arching, bare skin gliding hotly over bare skin.

"I love this," he gasped, running his hand under the leg of her teddy to cup her firm behind, while he wondered if she knew whether he meant the garment or her satiny flesh. He wasn't sure he knew himself.

When he felt her hands at his fly, fumbling with the buttons, he surged to a sitting position and gently moved them aside so he could deal with his boots and jeans. She turned away and he hurried, wanting to strip her himself. His fingers were like sausages, fat, clumsy and impatient. When he was finally done he turned—and froze.

She was gloriously naked. In the colorless light she glowed like a goddess carved from some fine, grainless wood as she lifted her hands to her hair. Her breasts jutted forward, so perfect he could have wept, the nipples beaded in the cool air. Only when he reached out a trembling finger to skim it down her throat and between her breasts, feeling the warmth of her skin, did the image dissolve into one of flesh, bone and welcoming heat.

She reached for him and his brain emptied of rational thought. His blood pooled lower, much lower, in his anatomy. His eyes may have crossed—he couldn't be sure. Still, he tried hard to hang on to his shredding control as he explored her intimately, tried until she whimpered, hands skimming over him with greedy intent.

The two of them sought and found each other, coming together with throaty cries, sighs of relief, groans of pleasure. He shook his head, trying to clear it, trying to focus on her and not his own urgent needs, but she pulled him closer, deeper, tighter.

He felt the tremors begin inside her, heard her moan. Something came loose within him. His heart leaped in his chest and he broke, a man driven past his limits. She arched against him and cried out. Helpless with it, he followed her over the edge.

She was too limp, too utterly boneless, to move, never mind to actually get up and find her clothes. He was half covering her, his breath whistling in her ear, his heart thudding against her breast.

"Are you okay?" he gasped when he could talk.

All she could manage was a satisfied "mmm."

His chuckle was weak, the stroke of his hand on her back a light yet proprietary caress. Then he gathered her close, and her heart stuttered, hoping for words, feelings, a sharing of minds.

Instead, he sighed and held her. She told herself it was enough for now.

She must have dozed; she woke when he shook her lightly.

"I don't want to, but I should take you home." His voice was a whisper, a drift of air in the darkness. The moon must have gone behind a cloud. He had the substance of a shadow.

Home? To take her home? She tried to gather her thoughts, but they dissolved like mist. "You want me to go?" she mumbled, struggling to rise.

His arm across her tightened like an iron bar. "No way, sweetheart. I just don't want to deal with your brother and pistols at dawn."

Despite the protest that rose in her throat, she could see the sense of it. Donovan took his role of big brother seriously.

"You're right," she whispered as she lifted a hand

and trailed it down the hard, flat muscles of J.D.'s chest. He shivered. Her nail scraped his nipple and she hesitated, exploring. Before she'd wandered far, he grabbed her wrist.

"Keep that up and I won't let you out of here for a week."

"Sounds good to me."

His grunt of laughter was endearing. "You don't know how much I'd like that," he muttered, and then he began searching for his clothes. She was sorting hers out in the dimness when he turned to her. "This isn't casual," he said, surprising her. "I'm not sure where we're headed, but it's not—I wouldn't do that to you."

Tears sprang to her eyes. Before she could answer, he leaned over and kissed her brow. Then his lips found hers and heat poured through her.

A little while later, he drove her up to the main house. The porch light was on, so he gave her a quick kiss before he helped her out.

"I'll see you tomorrow," he said.

She wanted to ask him when, how soon, but she bit back the question. They'd come a long way tonight and they both needed time to steady themselves before they moved on. She thanked him again for dinner, wondering how much of what she was feeling was there in her eyes for him to read, and then let herself into the house as quietly as possible. When he eased the pickup into gear, she stood in the open door and waved. He waved back and then drove down the road. She watched until his taillights disappeared.

"Did you have a good time?" Bobbie asked from the gloom of the hallway.

Kirby uttered a little squeak of surprise.

"I wasn't waiting in ambush," Bobbie added hastily as she came into the kitchen. The light over the stove was on, and Kirby saw she was wearing a dark robe with braid trim. "I was getting some water and I thought I heard the truck. I didn't mean to startle you."

Kirby wondered if the activities of the last couple of hours showed on her face, like a glowing brand. Had she combed her hair? No doubt her lip gloss had been nibbled off, her mascara left on the pillowcase.

"I had a nice time," she said. "J.D. has signed a contract for his woodwork with a gallery from Aspen. That's what we were celebrating." She hoped she wasn't revealing anything he didn't want made public. He hadn't said and she hadn't thought to ask, but he was so intensely private that it was hard for her to know for sure.

Bobbie set down the water glass she'd been filling. "Didn't you say your brother from Boise has a gallery? In Aspen?" she demanded suspiciously.

Kirby nodded.

"Does J.D. know?"

She shook her head. "He would never have accepted Jonathan's help if he did. You know how stubborn J.D. can be."

"Oh, honey," Bobbie groaned, "what have you done? You know you've got to tell him the truth."

"Not yet." There was no way Kirby could do that just now. "Later on, when he believes in himself, I'll tell him everything. I promise. He'll understand."

Bobbie's brow was furrowed with worry. "I pray that you're right, but if he finds out you've tricked him, I'm afraid he may have a hard time forgiving you."

Because her sister-in-law's fears echoed Kirby's own, she shook her head vehemently, as if she could ward them off that way.

She loved him, she realized. She couldn't risk losing him, and it was too late to tell him about Jonathan. Way too late.

"I wrote a letter this morning." Kirby had the day off, and she was leaning against the fence of a small corral behind the stable, watching J.D. working his filly. It was a cold, clear day, the mountains to the west marching across the horizon like icy sentinels. Her breath puffed out in a small, white cloud as if she were smoking a cigarette.

J.D. glanced over his shoulder, his long hair brushing the turned-up collar of his jacket beneath his ever-present cowboy hat. He still made her heart pound like a cattle stampede. "Who did you write to?"

For a moment she didn't answer. Instead she feasted on him as memories of the evening before, when they had again been together, stirred her senses. Mmm, but he looked good, with his long legs sheathed in tight denim, spurs jangling when he moved.

He'd had some moves the night before, as well. For the last couple of weeks they'd spent whatever time they could manage together. Donovan, bless his heart, had wisely kept his mouth shut about Kirby's frequent absences, although she suspected it wasn't easy for him to sit across from her at supper every evening and not comment. Perhaps little Rose's presence deterred him.

"When I grow up, I'm going to marry J.D.," Rose had announced at the table one evening.

"You'll probably change your mind several times before then," Bobbie replied with a glance at Kirby.

She had to admire the five-year-old for staking her claim so clearly as Kirby wondered how to explain to her niece what she didn't fully understand herself—where her own relationship with him was headed.

"I wrote to the Wilsons, my adopted parents," she told J.D. now. The letter had been short, only a couple of pages describing the ranch and her work as a visiting nurse. She'd avoided accusations or questions about anything controversial.

"How'd that make you feel?" he asked as he ran his hands over the filly's back and rump. He'd told her before that it was important the horse become comfortable with being touched and handled. While he did, Kirby could hear him whisper, the sound like a cat's purr. A delicious shiver ran through her and she looked around. There wasn't another soul in sight.

"Come over here and I'll tell you how I feel," she invited, slipping through the rails of the fence so she was standing inside the corral.

J.D. arched a brow. Then he grinned and sauntered over to her, the loose-limbed roll of his hips nearly hiding his limp. His hat was pulled low over his eyes and his arms dangled at his sides, reminding her of a fighter stalking his opponent.

"You lonesome, little lady?" he asked, pushing back the brim of his Stetson as he stood over her.

Kirby swallowed a chuckle at his playacting, thrilled to see emerging a side of him that she'd never suspected. Part of it was due, she knew, to the shot of confidence and purpose his contract with Jonathan gave him. Part, perhaps, to the relationship growing between him and herself.

"I'm lonesome for you," she murmured, gaze locked on his as she sidled even closer, until their bodies were touching. She slipped her hands under the edges of his open jacket and rested them on his chest. Beneath her palm, his heart beat out a slow, steady rhythm.

Last night she'd felt it hammering as if it were about to explode. Greedily, she wanted to feel it pumping out of control again. Nuzzling her hips even closer, she tipped back her head and gazed at him through her lashes.

"You're asking for trouble," he warned, but his lips were curved.

"Have I found it yet?" Her voice was throaty, nearly making her cough. Deliberately, she sucked in a breath, thrusting out her breasts, and ran her tongue across her lower lip.

His eyes narrowed and she glimpsed a flash of predatory intent cross his features, disappearing again so quickly she wasn't sure she hadn't imagined it.

With a low groan, he swept her into his arms. "You found it." His mouth skimmed up her throat, and then she felt the edge of his teeth on her earlobe. His breath tickled her ear and he shook her once, hard, while she grabbed for his shoulders. "Look at me like that again and I'll take you right here on the ground."

The beat of Kirby's pulse tripled at the raw hunger in his voice. Her hands crept around his neck. "But it's so cold."

Eyes glittering like obsidian, he let her slide down his body. Then he anchored her close with his arm and pressed the straining bulge of his arousal against her stomach. "I'm not cold, city girl."

Neither was she. Perhaps a deserted stall, she mused with the part of her brain still capable of producing a coherent thought. Then, over the sound of her own pulse slamming in her ears, she heard whistling.

J.D. must have heard it, too. His kiss was firm but way too brief. Then he released her and stepped back, just as Charlie came around the corner.

"Hi, y'all," he said in greeting as he kept going toward the stable. "Sorry I'm late, J.D. I'll start cleaning stalls now."

"I 'ppreciate it," J.D. drawled with a crooked grin. As soon as Charlie disappeared again, he held up a warning hand. "No more of that while I'm on the clock," he told her.

"Afraid I'll sidetrack you?" she asked.

"I know damn well you will. Now tell me about this letter you wrote. Are you going to make up with your folks?"

The question distracted her most effectively. She pursed her lips while she thought about the answer. "I'm not ready for that, but I guess they deserve to know I'm okay."

J.D. smiled his approval, and her breath left her in a whoosh.

"I'm glad to hear it," he said as he returned his attention to the filly. "Don't you feel better, now that you've done it?"

She wasn't sure how to answer and found herself mouthing a vague platitude that seemed to satisfy him. Over the next few days, she thought about it often. How did she feel? She'd cared about them most of her life; could one lie destroy all the love they'd shown her over the years? As Jonathan had told her, their intentions had been good, even if they were misguided. Was she so perfect that she couldn't forgive them for one error in judgment?

No, she realized, her stomach lurching uncomfortably as she thought of the truth she was withholding from J.D. Hadn't her parents' intentions—to protect her—been as noble as her own were now? When he found out what *she* had done, would he feel as betrayed as she had, or would he understand and forgive, as she herself had so far refused to do?

Chapter Eleven

"You wanted to see me?" J.D. shoved his hands into his back pockets, shoulders braced, and watched Buchanan nail a new railing onto the chute they used to sort cattle for branding and vaccinations. When J.D. had ridden in from the range where he'd been exercising one of the horses, he'd been told the boss was looking for him. J.D.'s gut had been tense ever since.

Had he finally gone too far? Was Buchanan going to warn him away from Kirby or just flat-out fire him?

At the sound of his voice, Buchanan glanced up and grinned. Then he brought the hammer down again and let out a yelp. "Dammit!" he exclaimed, yanking off his glove to jam the injured thumb into his mouth. "That hurt."

"Do you want ice to put on it?" J.D. figured

Cookie down at the bunkhouse would have some in his fridge.

Buchanan's expression was sheepish beneath his baseball cap. "Naw, don't bother. I didn't hit it that hard." He waved his injured hand around. "It'll be okay."

J.D. waited for him to get to whatever was eating at him. Instead he gave his hand a final shake, shoved it back into his glove and flexed it a couple of times experimentally.

"Hold the other end of this board for me, would you?"

J.D. did as he asked while Buchanan tapped the nail in place. When he was done, he threaded the hammer through a loop on the carpenter's belt he wore and leaned against the chute. "What's on your mind?"

"Gus said you were looking for me," J.D. replied, stomach tightening another notch.

"Oh, that's right." Buchanan glanced around at the rail he'd been repairing. "How about we go down to the kitchen and talk Cookie out of a cup of coffee? Everyone else is out riding fence."

J.D. shrugged, careful to keep any trace of concern from showing on his face. If Buchanan had a problem with him, he'd have to lay it out.

By the time they'd seated themselves with coffee and a plate of freshly baked cookies, J.D. was beginning to wonder if he'd jumped to the wrong conclusion. Buchanan was as affable as ever; if he was angry about Kirby or anything else, he hid it behind a poker face.

"Any problems with the horses?" he asked now, after he'd added sugar to his mug and stirred it several times. He'd removed his gloves, and the thumb he'd smashed was still red.

"Naw, everything's pretty much on schedule." J.D. tried not to fidget. Instead, he took a sip of his own coffee and burned his tongue. If he had to leave the Rocking Rose, so be it, but he wasn't about to give Kirby up. Not now. She was like a drug in his veins; he couldn't get enough of her.

"Hessinger, that buyer from Nebraska, called to let me know how pleased he is with the horses he bought for reining. Said they're trained better than just about anything he's ever had." Buchanan's grin etched creases into his weathered skin. Except for his yellow hair, several shades lighter than Kirby's, and his green eyes, he might have passed as a blood brother of J.D.'s.

J.D. wondered how Buchanan had felt when he first saw Kirby after being apart for so many years, but he couldn't ask. Part of him longed for family of his own. A couple of siblings might have been nice.

"Hessinger threatened to offer you a job on his spread," Buchanan continued as J.D. tried to recall what they'd been discussing. Oh, the guy from Nebraska.

"As what?" he asked dryly.

"Horse trainer," Buchanan said around a mouthful of oatmeal cookie. "I told you he was impressed with Star and Babyface."

J.D. looked out the window at the bleak scenery. "Nebraska's too damned cold."

The other man's grin widened. "I'm glad you feel that way."

"Why?" J.D. asked.

Buchanan sobered and searched J.D.'s face. "You

know, I would have hired you anyway, if I'd had any clue how good with horses you are," he said quietly. "It's not just because of the accident that I keep you on here. You've more than earned the job."

J.D.'s eyes widened, but he said nothing. Instead, he took another sip of coffee, but his gaze never left Buchanan's. The green eyes didn't waver.

"It's not some misguided sense of gratitude that's kept me from talking to you about my sister, either."

At the mention of Kirby, J.D. stiffened. "I wouldn't hurt her," he said, surprising himself. He didn't owe anyone an explanation of his intentions. Then he reminded himself that Buchanan was new at this big-brother stuff. It wouldn't hurt to cut him a little slack.

"Oh, I think I figured that out. You're in love with her, aren't you?"

If J.D. had been on horseback he'd probably have fallen off. Automatically, he opened his mouth to deny it. Then he dropped his gaze to his coffee mug, tilting it this way and that. "I don't know." He thought about asking if she'd confided her feelings to her brother, then discarded the idea. He wouldn't say, if she had.

"Having been there myself, I can understand. Just take damn good care of her until you decide." Buchanan drained his mug and finished his cookie. His eyes glinted. "You got that?"

J.D. got the message loud and clear. As if he needed it. "I'd kill the man who took advantage of her," he said fervently. "If she didn't beat me to it."

Buchanan's brows rose in obvious surprise, and then he chuckled as he got to his feet. This time when he slapped him on the back, J.D. didn't flinch away

from the contact. "I think we understand each other."
Buchanan stuck out his hand.

J.D. hesitated only for a moment. Then he gave it
a firm shake as he got up from the table. "I guess we
do. If there isn't anything else, I've got work to do."
The tightness in his stomach had started to ease up.

"Me, too. I need to finish that railing." Buchanan
picked up the two mugs and the plate and headed for
the kitchen. When he was halfway there, he turned.
"You can talk to me anytime."

"Thanks." As J.D. went back outside, he knew he
wouldn't take him up on his offer. His grandfather
had taught him to work things out for himself.

He crossed the yard, mulling over what Buchanan
had said about his job. Was it possible that he'd mis-
judged Donovan? J.D. thought back to when the two
of them had been on the circuit, competing head-to-
head in the PRCA standings. No matter how many
times he'd ignored Buchanan, the other man had always acknowledged him with a nod or a grin. J.D.
used to think he was just thickheaded; now he wondered.

It could have been anyone's kid J.D. had shoved
from the path of that speeding truck. He was no hero;
he'd acted on instinct and he hadn't expected to ben-
efit from it. Neither would he whine about what it had
cost him.

Pride had forced him to refuse Buchanan's offer of
settling his medical bills. He paid his own way. Pride
had choked him when he'd been forced to accept the
job Buchanan crammed down his gullet. Now pride
made him reconsider.

He was good at what he did. Gratitude might have
opened the door, but he'd earned the right to stay.

J.D. wondered if Kirby had said anything to her brother about the deal for his woodworking. He should have told Buchanan himself and assured him it wouldn't cut into his time with the horses. Hell, he thought, bending down to pick up a small rock in the path and toss it aside, Buchanan trusted him with Rose and with Kirby. No doubt he trusted J.D. to give him a day's work for a day's pay, as well.

It was a good feeling, being trusted.

Normally, Kirby would have loved spending time with J.D. in his workshop, helping him to decide on a design for the new oak headboard he was planning. Outside, the snow was coming down thick and fast. She didn't have to work today, the horses were taken care of and Donovan and his family were visiting friends in Denver until tomorrow. They'd invited her to go along, but she'd begged off. They needed time to themselves and she wanted to be with J.D.

Now if guilt would quit nibbling at the edges of her conscience, she'd be fine. Next week was Thanksgiving, and Ashley had called to insist she invite J.D. along. Donovan seconded the idea. After a slight hesitation, J.D. had agreed to go.

Now the two of them had the rest of the day to spend together. When they were done here, she was going to cook for them—nothing complicated, just steak, baked potatoes, salad, and ice cream for dessert. Then J.D. would lead her upstairs and take her into his arms—

"What do you think of this?" he asked, breaking into her pleasant dream to hold up a rough sketch of a geometric design. It reminded her of a pattern she'd seen on handwoven rugs.

She tilted her head, considering. "I like it." When she glanced up, she saw that he was watching her intently. "Really, I do."

Very deliberately, he set the paper he was holding down on the workbench. Then he hooked an arm around her waist and tugged until she was flush against him.

"How long will dinner take to prepare?"

She wrinkled her nose thoughtfully. "Maybe a half hour. Why?"

His attention settled on her mouth. "Are you starving?"

Kirby's breath backed up in her throat as she felt his body stir against hers. "N-not really. Are you?"

He grinned, exposing his white teeth as he leaned closer. His voice dropped to a rough whisper. "Guess."

When Kirby woke up later in J.D.'s bed, cuddled close to him, she looked over her shoulder into his face. His narrowed eyes were focused on a spot somewhere on the far wall. She shifted, with the intent of nibbling on his bare chest, but he tightened his arms and looked down at her with a serious expression.

"What are you thinking?" she asked, as alarm filtered through her happy glow.

"Thinking about what I'm going to do when the headboard is finished. Do you have any idea what this contract with the gallery means?"

Kirby's conscience gave another painful tweak. "I think so."

Jamming a pillow behind his head, he pulled himself up to a sitting position and plucked at the blanket with his fingers. "It's a chance to—I don't know—

to control my own destiny again, I guess. This job with your brother was handed to me because of something that happened, a twist of fate. But the carving is *mine*. Whether I succeed or fail at it depends entirely on me." He thumped his bare chest with his fist. "I don't owe anyone," he added, a muscle jumping in his cheek. "My skill with wood got me this opportunity, not some freak accident, not someone's sense of obligation. Do you understand what I'm trying to say?"

"Yes, I do." What he was saying, she realized with a sharp pang, was that his pride would force him to back out of the agreement he had with Jonathan if she told him what she'd done. Right or wrong, she was stuck with the situation, at least for now. Her biggest hope was that when the time came to tell him, J.D. would be so deeply involved with her that he'd have no choice but to forgive her for her deception. Until then, there was no point in dwelling on something she could do nothing to change.

"Hungry?" she asked, shoving aside her worries and glancing at the clock on his nightstand. It was hard to believe that they had loved away the entire afternoon. J.D. had taken her higher and higher, like a man possessed, finding his own satisfaction only when she finally begged him to join her in the fiery conflagration.

Exhausted, they had fallen asleep in each other's arms. After a short nap, he had carried her into the nearby shower, where he bathed her with tender consideration and wrapped her in a towel. Bringing her back to the bedroom, he had loved her again with devastating thoroughness, until she came apart in his arms with his name on her lips.

When she'd recovered from his ministrations, she turned on him, determined to show him what she didn't yet dare to say—how much she loved him. She managed to shatter his self-control with an intensity that left them both exhausted. Afterward, he fell asleep in her arms. Satiated and brimming with love, she had followed him into sweet oblivion.

"It was hunger that started this in the first place," he replied to her question now. Before he could say anything more, his stomach rumbled loudly, making them both laugh.

"I think my man needs feeding." Kirby sat up and reached for the clothes she'd stripped off much earlier.

"I wish you could move in with me," he said, surprising her.

Kirby stopped trying to turn her sweater right side out and stared. "You do?"

He leaned over and placed an openmouthed kiss on her bare stomach. His mouth was like an inferno. The rasp of his tongue on her skin sent a tremor of pleasure through her. "Does the idea bother you?" He slid closer, trailing kisses across the curve of her breast while he traced a pattern on her thigh with his fingers.

With little success, Kirby struggled against the tide of desire rising within her. In truth, living with him would be sheer heaven.

"I couldn't do that right under Donovan's nose," she said as logic lifted its ugly head.

"I know." His voice was gruff. Was he disappointed? He hadn't exactly asked her, had only said he wished she could.

How she longed for him to tell her how he felt.

Did he care for her or was he merely taking advantage of a woman willing to share his bed? Was she a fool to assume he couldn't treat her with such tender attention if his emotions weren't involved?

"I'm glad you understand," she told him, pulling her sweater over her head and fluffing out her hair.

"Doesn't mean I like it, though," he replied as he began donning his own clothes.

Kirby's heart soared at his gruff comment. He must have some feeling for her.

Later that week, the hope stayed with her as she helped Bobbie and Rose prepare for the Thanksgiving feast to come. Even though dinner was at Ashley and Taylor's this year, Bobbie had promised to bring the pies and a molded salad.

Kirby diced celery for the salad while Bobbie rolled out pie dough and Rose stirred up the ingredients for the pumpkin filling.

"You're awfully quiet," Bobbie commented after Rose had excused herself to go to the bathroom. "Problems?"

Kirby shook her head. "Just thinking about a patient." She crossed the fingers of one hand behind her back, unwilling to admit she was wondering what J.D. was doing at that very minute and wishing she could be with him. Despite her growing fondness for her new family, her feelings for J.D. were so precious that they seemed to fill every corner of her heart.

"I appreciate your help with all this," Bobbie said with a wave of her hand.

"No problem. I enjoy it." That, at least, wasn't a fib. When she'd been married, Kirby had enjoyed cooking. It was only after her divorce that she'd resorted to frozen entrées and fast food. Cooking for one seemed like a waste of time and only served to emphasize the loneliness of her life. Now, however, she was finding that the satisfaction of preparing food for her loved ones was both a comfort and a challenge.

The phone on the wall rang as Rose walked back into the room. "Can I answer that?" she asked her mother.

Bobbie raised one hand, amply dusted with flour. "No, honey. Let Aunt Kirby. You don't mind, do you?"

With a shake of her head, Kirby grabbed the receiver. "Hello?"

"Kirby, dear, it's so good to hear your voice," Marge Wilson said. "Your—Bob and I enjoyed your letter so much and we just wanted to wish you a happy Thanksgiving."

Despite Kirby's mixed emotions, the voice of the woman she'd thought of as her mother for over twenty years was soothing in its familiarity.

"Happy Thanksgiving to both of you," she replied. "How is everyone?"

"We're fine. Jonathan and Martin are flying in this morning and they'll be staying through the weekend. I wish you could have been here, but I figured you'd have other plans."

If there was a slight hint of rebuke in her tone, Kirby managed to ignore it. "We're all going to my older brother Taylor's, for dinner," she replied. "Right now I'm helping Bobbie and Rose with the pies."

"Are you making any mince?" Marge Wilson asked. "I know it's your favorite."

"Of course. What's Thanksgiving without mincemeat pie?"

"When are you coming home to Boise, dear? Your friends all miss you, and so do we. You know you're welcome anytime. You can stay in your old apartment over the garage whenever you like."

To her surprise, Kirby realized that she missed them, missed talking to Marge and seeing Jan and her other friends. Perhaps time was beginning to close old wounds, but she wasn't ready to leave J.D. or her brothers, not even for a short time, not yet.

"I'm not ready to come back," she said. "Maybe later on, but not now."

"If you'd rather, we could all meet in Aspen and visit with your brother," Marge Wilson suggested. "I understand you haven't been to see him, either."

"I haven't had time," Kirby replied. "But I will."

"We could come to Denver," her mother persisted. "I've never been there. We could sightsee. Whatever you want."

"I appreciate that, but I'm not sure right now," Kirby told her. Then she relented a little. "We can probably work out something, maybe during the Christmas holidays."

Over the line, she heard the older woman draw in a shaky breath, and Kirby felt bad, despite her own hurt.

"That's a wonderful idea, darling. I won't keep you now, but we'll talk again real soon."

After Kirby had said her goodbyes and broken the connection, she looked out the kitchen window for a long moment before she turned back to Bobbie.

"Everything okay?" her sister-in-law asked as she poured the pumpkin filling into two pans.

Briefly, Kirby explained who had been on the other end of the line and what they had discussed.

"How did that make you feel, talking to her?" Bobbie opened the oven door and slid in the pies.

"I guess I've been selfish," Kirby admitted as she shoved her hands into the pockets of her wool slacks. "Just thinking about myself and my own feelings. Today, most of all, I should be thinking about what I have, not looking for problems."

Bobbie smiled at her as Rose looked up from the scraps of cinnamon- and sugar-sprinkled dough that she was dotting with butter. "We're all thankful," Bobbie said quietly.

The sincerity of her tone brought sudden tears to Kirby's eyes. She was indeed a lucky woman.

She repeated as much to J.D. on the way back from Taylor's later that night. She was seated next to him in his pickup as he drove back through the dark, and they were both replete from the holiday meal.

Beside her on the bench seat, J.D. thought about the apparent ease with which her family had accepted him at their dinner table. At first, after grace had been said and bowls heaped with mashed potatoes, gravy, stuffing and other traditional holiday foods were being passed around, he'd felt self-conscious, despite the reassuring way Kirby squeezed his hand under the table. Eventually, though, the kidding and conversation that surrounded him had drawn him in. By the time his plate was loaded, Taylor's boys had begun pelting him with questions about his days in rodeo. Their dad had been a steer wrestler, one of the timed events, but it was easy to see that his sons were fascinated with bull riders.

Ashley, a retired barrel racer, had shared a few stories of her own about life on the road. Never easy, the grueling schedule must have been even tougher for women, J.D. realized, as she described her first meeting with her husband, when he and Donovan stopped to help her with a flat tire on a deserted road between rodeos.

"Did you quit to get married?" J.D. had asked her curiously.

Her reply, that a fall by her horse during competition and her resulting knee injury had forced her retirement, made him realize he wasn't the only one fate had dealt a difficult hand.

At least now she seemed happy with her family, and J.D. had the promise of a new career. And perhaps a chance for happiness with the woman sitting beside him in his pickup. Maybe fate did give second chances to those who weren't afraid to reach out and try.

In the dim light from the dash, he covered Kirby's hand with his. "Did you have a good time?" he asked.

She sighed and patted her stomach. "I should have skipped dessert. Other than feeling as if I'll never have to eat again, I'm fine. How about you? Did you enjoy yourself? I hope you didn't feel like you were being interviewed for an exposé."

"You have a nice family," he replied, realizing that he meant what he said. "I didn't mind the questions."

She squeezed his hand. "I agree, they are pretty nice."

It wasn't until later, after they'd made love in his bed and he'd walked her back through the cold evening air to her brother's house, that J.D. realized something was different between the two of them. This time, when they'd come together, it felt to him as if they had shared more than their bodies. It had been as if their hearts, even their souls, had somehow touched. He wondered whether he was only being fanciful or if Kirby, too, had noticed the difference, but he didn't know how to ask. Perhaps if his new career took off and he had something real to offer, he'd be able to ask how she really felt about him. Meanwhile, these stolen moments together would have to be enough.

He dropped her hand and put his arm around her shoulder as she smiled up at him. For the first time in a long while, he felt as though he had a lot to be thankful for.

December seemed to be made up of one snowstorm after another, Kirby mused as she stared out the window. She had gotten up before dawn this morning because J.D. was delivering some finished pieces to Jonathan in Aspen and had asked her to ride along with him. Donovan was loaning them the ranch truck with four-wheel drive, and they were setting out in less than half an hour. Her brother wasn't up yet and Bobbie had a cold. Reluctantly, Kirby had offered to stay with Rose, but Donovan had promised to come back to the house in time to get her up and ready for school so that Bobbie could stay in bed.

Too excited at the idea of spending the entire day with J.D., and seeing Jonathan, to sleep, Kirby had been awake for a couple of hours. She wore a ski sweater with a red-white-and-navy pattern over warm blue slacks, and her red parka was hanging by the back door. Her gloves were stuffed in the pocket.

On the table were the roast-beef-and-tomato sandwiches she'd packed, along with brownies and a thermos of coffee. Aspen was four hours southwest of Denver, so they wouldn't be back until tonight.

At the sound of an engine breaking the silence of the early morning, Kirby slipped into her coat and grabbed the lunch sack and her purse. J.D. was behind the wheel of the shiny black truck. In the back, his wood pieces were carefully packed and covered by a tarp.

When she emerged from the house, he climbed down from the cab. He was wearing a baseball cap, Wranglers and his cowboy boots, plus his heavy jacket over a plaid wool shirt.

"I missed you last night," he said as he took her into his arms. Since Thanksgiving he'd been much more openly affectionate, as if he no longer worried what anyone else thought of their relationship. Or as if his feelings for her were growing.

"I'm glad you missed me," she replied as he lowered his head. His lips were cool when they touched hers, but they heated quickly.

Despite their heavy clothing, Kirby could feel the warmth of his body as she pressed against him. The day before she'd been on several nursing calls and he'd been to Greeley to pick up a horse, so she'd seen him only for an hour in the evening. Now she held him tightly, savoring his nearness.

All too soon, he broke the kiss. "I dreamed about you," she confessed, keeping her arms around his waist.

He nuzzled her hair. "Was it a good dream?"

"Mmm-hmm. We were somewhere warm, with a white, sandy beach and lots of palm trees." She didn't add that neither of them had been wearing anything but plain gold rings. That part of the fantasy was still too private to share.

J.D. helped her into the truck. "I hope we weren't dressed like we are now," he said as he climbed in after her and fastened both their seat belts. "It would be a damned shame to cover up your body for no good reason."

His comment and the way he eyed her made Kirby flush with pleasure. She was tempted to admit they hadn't been wearing a stitch, but then he might ask what they were doing in the dream and she couldn't tell him they'd been on their honeymoon. He'd think she was hinting about a commitment.

Instead, she changed the subject as they drove down the road and turned onto the main highway. After a couple of hours they stopped to stretch their legs, and J.D. checked the load.

"I hope the weatherman was right and we don't get any snow before we get home," he said as he cast a concerned look at the sky. Its gray expanse was so pale it was nearly colorless, but at least there weren't any storm clouds in sight.

After a quick snack of coffee and brownies, they were back on the road. Kirby offered to take a turn behind the wheel, but J.D. suggested she wait until the return trip. Right before they got to Aspen, they stopped again to eat the sandwiches she'd packed and finish the coffee.

"Do you have directions to the gallery?" she asked when J.D. pulled back onto Highway 82. She hadn't been to the gallery since right after Jonathan and Martin had first opened it, but she remembered how to get there. It was on the most fashionable street in town, sitting between an exclusive skiwear boutique and a high-priced restaurant where she'd been thrilled to see the star of a popular television series.

J.D. took a folded paper from his pocket. "He gave me directions over the phone. Care to navigate?"

"Sure." She read through the written instructions, relieved to see that they would indeed take them right to Jonathan's shop. When she'd talked to her brother the night before, reminding him that he mustn't give her away, he'd said his partner would be out of town on a buying trip today. They'd be alone except for a young clerk Kirby hadn't met.

Eventually, J.D. pulled up behind the gallery. After she'd gone through the uncomfortable pretext of being introduced to her own brother, suffering fresh guilt pangs, J.D. left the two of them while he went out to bring in the headboard and the other pieces he'd brought with them.

Kirby waited until she was sure he was gone before she turned back to Jonathan, who was watching her with a worried frown.

"I can't thank you enough for doing this," she told him quietly. "Because of you, J.D.'s already starting to act differently, more confident in himself."

"He's talented," Jonathan assured her. "Martin agrees with me. If you didn't know Mr. Reese from Adam I'd still be thrilled to handle his work. Good Western art is very hot and there's a huge market for what he's doing. All we have to do is tap into it and I predict he'll be in demand."

His praise eased some of Kirby's guilt, because she knew Jonathan would never exaggerate. She hoped it wouldn't be long before she could tell J.D. the truth.

All she had to do was to figure out how.

"How was your visit with Mom and Dad?" she asked, amazed at how easily the familiar terms of address rolled off her tongue. It was no use; as hurt as she was, Bob and Marge Wilson were still the only parents she could remember.

Jonathan glanced around cautiously and then said, "Mom told me that she'd called you. I'm glad you seem to be patching things up. She said you discussed getting together during the holidays, and she was really excited about the idea." His expression was anxious. "I'm sure they only did what they thought was best."

Reluctant to go back over old ground, Kirby merely nodded. "I haven't forgiven them," she said, "but I'm starting to miss Boise a little more." She pressed her hand to his cheek. "No matter what else happens, you'll always be my brother."

Jonathan's cheeks flushed with pleasure. "And you, dear one, will always be my favorite sister." His arms closed around her in a quick hug and then he stepped back.

"Don't you mean your only sister?" she teased.

"Don't you think you'd better explain the relationship to me?" came a voice from behind them. "I seem to have missed something along the way." J.D. walked out from the back room with a grim expression on his lean face. "It seems my introductions were unnecessary."

His anger was nearly palpable. There was no doubt he'd heard way too much for Kirby to be able to cover up her blunder. All she could do was tell him the truth and hope he wasn't too upset to listen.

"Don't blame her for this," Jonathan said, stepping in front of her protectively before she could utter a word. "She was only trying to help you. I was just telling her I'd have bought your work even if she didn't know you."

"Don't you mean even if she wasn't sleeping with me?" J.D. sneered as Kirby muffled a gasp. Then he turned on her. An angry red flush ran beneath the skin stretched taut across his cheekbones. "I must be pretty damned good in the sack for you to go to this much trouble."

Embarrassment, regret and genuine fear whipped through Kirby as she confronted him. "You don't understand," she cried, her heart breaking at the bleakness she saw in his eyes. "I only wanted to help, and I knew you'd never accept it."

"So you decided to force it on me anyway." Flexing his hands as if he couldn't quite control them, he jammed them onto his hips. "Tell me," he demanded. "Was the idea of an affair with a horse trainer so distasteful that you had to pretty me up? Why didn't you just go after some other sucker in the first place?"

She knew he was talking this way because he felt betrayed, but his words still hurt like a knife slicing through her. She glanced at her brother, who was watching both of them with indecision on his face. He was barely her height and slight of build, but she was still afraid he'd do something foolish in a misguided attempt to defend her.

"Jonnie, would you leave us alone for a minute?" she pleaded.

Obviously indecisive, he glanced at J.D. and then back to her. He'd tried to warn her that this might happen. "Are you sure?"

She knew that no matter how angry he was, J.D.

would never physically harm her. He wasn't that kind of man. "Of course I am."

"Don't bother," J.D. said before Jonathan could exit. "We're leaving right now and I'm taking my stuff back with me." He made a slashing motion with his hand. "As of right now, our agreement is dissolved."

"Oh, please don't do this," Kirby cried. It was much worse than she'd feared. In striking back at her, he was hurting himself as well.

"Wait," Jonathan said. "I'm afraid things aren't that simple." His obstinate expression as he faced J.D. was one Kirby was intimately familiar with. "You signed an exclusive contract with us that covers anything you make from wood. If you don't honor it, I'll make sure the only places you sell your work are flea markets and garage sales."

J.D. went pale and then his eyes glittered dangerously. "That suits me just fine," he growled between clenched teeth. Then he directed his diamond-hard gaze at Kirby. "Lady, if you don't want to take the bus back to your *other* brother's, you'd better get your butt out to my pickup pronto."

With a last angry glance at Jonathan, he spun on his heel and stalked out the door.

"I'll talk to him," Kirby promised. "He'll calm down when he's had a chance to think this through."

"I'm sorry, sis," Jonathan replied with a rueful shake of his head, "but I don't think he's going to forgive either of us for this little charade—at least not anytime in the near future."

Chapter Twelve

Hurt and fury still churning inside him, J.D. wanted nothing more than to put a fist through the wall. Instead he slammed out the rear entrance to the gallery and jerked open the door of the truck. Before he could climb in, Kirby hurried out after him.

"J.D., wait! Let me explain."

Ignoring her pleas, he stood back so she could slide behind the wheel, and indicated with a jab of his hand that she should do so. When she hesitated, he chanced a look at her. It was a mistake.

Her eyes were swimming with unshed tears and her face was pale. Her lips were trembling, and part of him wanted to crush them with his own in a punishing kiss. Instead, he said coldly, "Get in."

If she didn't comply, he was nearly furious enough to drive off without her.

Something in his face must have convinced her that

any further argument would be futile. With one glance at the tarp-covered load in the back of the truck, she brushed past him and scrambled into the cab.

The trip back to the ranch seemed to take forever. He spoke to her only twice, to ask if she needed a bathroom. When she nodded each time, he pulled over. When she came back out at the second stop, a busy truckstop and minimart, he'd brought coffee and a couple packages of cookies back to the pickup.

"Thank you," she murmured when he handed her a cup of the steaming coffee and a bag of Oreos. She drank her coffee in silence, huddled on the seat as he started the truck and left the parking lot, but he noticed that she didn't touch the cookies.

For the first time since he'd overheard her and Wilson, J.D. felt a twinge of conscience in the midst of his anger. Turning onto the main road, he wanted to ask her why she had deceived him, but he didn't know if he was really ready to listen to what she might say. Did she think him so weak that he needed her to go behind his back like this?

Without looking her way, he turned on the radio. A rowdy country tune helped fill the silence in the cab. After what seemed like hours, he felt a soft bump against his shoulder. Kirby had fallen asleep.

It was the last time Kirby had slept soundly in the week since they'd been back from Aspen. Twice she tried to talk to J.D., confronting him first at his house and then at the stable. Both times, he listened dispassionately to her plea for forgiveness without comment. When she was standing on his porch he shut the door in her face; in the stable, he mounted Buck's bare back and rode away.

"I don't know what to do," she told Bobbie as the two of them fixed supper late one afternoon. "He won't even talk to me."

"Honey, that's understandable. His pride's been hurt and he needs time." Bobbie gave her a quick hug and then went back to slicing carrots. "If he loves you, and I think he does, the two of you will work through this. I know the waiting is tough, but just be patient and give him some space."

"That's just it," Kirby admitted with a sniffle. "I don't know if he loves me or not. He's never said anything and now I'm afraid I've lost him for good." As the tears started to dribble down her cheeks, she made an excuse and hurried from the kitchen, nearly mowing down Rose on the staircase in her dash to the privacy of her bedroom.

The family had been very supportive. Donovan had even offered to talk to J.D., but Kirby made him swear that he wouldn't. Bobbie was probably right. If J.D. cared for her—Kirby didn't quite have the nerve to use the word *love* even to herself—they would somehow work things out. If he didn't, then perhaps it was time to accept the loss and start putting the pieces of her life back together. It wasn't as if she'd never had to do it before.

The only good that had come of all this was that she finally understood just how her parents could have kept the information about her adoption from her. Since she was guilty of the same thing—withholding the truth from someone out of love—it hadn't seemed at all fair not to forgive them. She'd written a long letter to them a couple of days before, suggesting they get together either in Idaho or here in Colorado, if they were still interested.

J.D. was brushing Buck, a chore that usually freed his mind whenever he had a problem to think through. Today it wasn't working.

The question that kept running through his tangled thoughts like a rat through a maze was how could Kirby have betrayed him the way she had? Didn't she see that taking charity from her former brother, or whatever the hell he was to her now, wasn't any different to J.D. than taking it from the Buchanans? In the time they'd spent together, in bed and out, hadn't she started figuring out what made him tick? Didn't she understand how important it had become to him to find something he'd earned for himself? Since the accident, he needed that more than ever, he thought as he yanked the comb through Buck's tail.

It caught on a snarl of hair. When he tugged at it impatiently, the horse snorted and shifted away from him.

"Sorry, boy," J.D. said aloud with a slap on the buckskin rump.

"Hi, J.D. Can I help you?" Rose asked from behind him as he nearly jumped out of his boots.

He'd been so preoccupied that he hadn't even heard her approach. His first impulse was to tell her the last thing he needed was company. Instead, he took a deep breath and dragged up a smile from the depths of his soul.

"Sure, honey. I can always use your help."

Rose slipped through the stall door and sat down on an overturned bucket in the corner. "I miss you," she said artlessly. "You stay by yourself all the time and you haven't been up to my house even once."

He knew her accusations were true. He'd been avoiding the main house, waiting until he saw Buchanan elsewhere if he needed to discuss anything with him. Once or twice he'd caught the other man studying him, but the boss kept his opinions, if he had any, to himself. J.D. wondered if Kirby had confided in him, and almost wished he had someone to talk to as well.

It was times like these that he missed his grandfather the most.

"I guess I've had a lot to think about," he told Rose as she swung her legs back and forth.

"About Christmas?" she guessed.

He'd nearly forgotten, but Christmas was only a little over a week away. "That and other things," he replied as he began picking out Buck's hooves.

"You're mad at Aunt Kirby, aren't you?"

"How'd you know that?" Was the news of their disagreement all over the ranch?

"I heard her and Mommy talking in the kitchen. They didn't know I was there."

With difficulty, J.D. bit back the urge to pump Rose for whatever she might know. To ask her how Kirby was doing. He'd been trying to convince himself he just didn't care, but with limited success.

"Don't you love Aunt Kirby anymore?" Rose asked.

He gawked at her, mouth open. How had a child figured out what it had taken him so long to admit to himself? He did love Kirby—with an intensity that made him ache—now that it was too late to do anything about it. Did everyone know what a fool he'd been to fall for a woman who couldn't accept him for what he was?

Hell, what did one more blow to his pride matter at this point?

"Yeah, I still love her," he said. "But you have to promise me not to tell her I said so, you understand?"

Rose bobbed her head, golden curls bouncing. "I promise. If you love her, why are you mad at her? It makes her cry. I hear her in her room sometimes when I'm walking by."

Pain ripped through him at the thought of those green cat's eyes shedding tears over him. He'd never meant to hurt her; in truth, he hadn't realized that he could.

"Sometimes love isn't enough," he said now, wondering if he was talking way over Rose's head.

"Love means never having to say you're sorry," she quoted loftily. "I saw that on television and it's true."

J.D. leaned against the wall of the stall and looked down at her. "You know some things on TV are make-believe, don't you?"

She nodded. "But you shouldn't make her cry. She must love you, too, and I bet she's sorry for whatever she did to make you mad. I cry sometimes, when Mommy or Daddy is mad at me. Then I feel lots better when they're not mad anymore."

J.D. mulled over what she'd said. What good would it do if he and Kirby made up? He'd never know how she really felt about who he was. What if his carving never went anywhere and all he ever had was this job or one just like it? How could he go on if she got fed up and left him? As much pain as he felt now, he knew it would be a hundred times worse if they got back together and he was constantly waiting for something like that to happen. Better to leave things the way they were.

"Sometimes a situation's more complicated than you can understand," he told Rose. "It isn't always enough to say you're sorry. You have to do something to show the person you're sincere."

Rose's forehead was creased with tiny wrinkles and her nose was scrunched up as she thought over what he'd said. "All I know is I miss you when I don't see you," she said finally. "It must be worse for Aunt Kirby, knowing you're here with the horses when she wants you to be with her instead."

When Kirby got back from her rounds two days later, Donovan came out the back door to meet her. It was snowing, the flakes floating down like feathers, and she was proud of herself for being able to go out alone. Since she and J.D. had returned from Aspen, there had been no question of him driving her, and Charlie had been too busy hauling feed to the cattle herd.

A shiver of fear went through her when she saw the expression on Donovan's face. Had something happened? A ranch could be a dangerous place. Had J.D. been hurt?

"What is it?" she demanded as Donovan came over and took her gloved hands in his. "Tell me."

"It's J.D.," he said, watching her intently. "I'm afraid I have some bad news."

Suddenly, Kirby felt cold all over. "He's hurt," she guessed, voice rising. "Oh, God. I have to go to him."

Donovan shook his head, and a shaft of pure terror sliced her heart.

"He's not—oh, God, he isn't—" She couldn't say the word.

Donovan's hands tightened on hers. "No, honey," he said, shaking his head vehemently. "Don't even think that. He's okay. It's just that he gave me his notice this morning."

Relief surged through her, followed closely by a wave of fresh anguish. J.D. was leaving the ranch.

"How soon is he going?" she asked. Had he given a week's notice? Two? As stubborn as he was, neither gave her much time to try to get through to him.

"He's leaving this afternoon," Donovan told her quietly, letting go of her hand to put a bracing arm around her shoulders. "I tried to stall him, but he's determined. I was watching for you, wondering what I'd do if he tried to leave before you got back."

The blood drained from her head so swiftly that she felt dizzy and sick to her stomach. "Today?" she whispered. "He's leaving today?"

Her brother's expression was grim. "I went down there a little while ago. He's packing as we speak."

To stifle a whimper, she pressed her knuckles to her mouth. Then a tiny spark of determination flickered, glowing faintly within her.

How dare J.D. even think about leaving without saying anything to her? How dare he slink away like a cowardly reptile.

She glanced down the road in the direction of J.D.'s house. "We'll just see about that."

Donovan held up a detaining hand. "Now, sis."

Getting angrier by the second, Kirby brushed past him and yanked open the door of her Bronco. "I've got a couple of things to say to the man before he even thinks about taking off,'' she said through clenched teeth as she slid behind the wheel. ''That's all.'' Leaving her brother standing in the yard with a worried look on his face, she floored the Bronco.

When she pulled up in front of J.D.'s house, she saw that he had an old canopy on the back of his pickup. Through its open back door, she could see that the bed was partly filled with furniture and cardboard boxes.

Bracing herself for a confrontation, Kirby got out of her Bronco and slammed the door, surprised to see the dog, Snake, standing at the base of the steps instead of hidden in his usual place beneath the porch.

As soon as he recognized her, Snake let out a bark of welcome that sounded more like the friendly greeting of a half-grown pup. His tail began to wag and he darted halfway over to where she stood staring before he hesitated. She extended a tentative hand, but he ignored it. Glancing instead at the house, he barked again.

Could he be worried that J.D. would leave him behind?

''Don't worry, boy,'' she found herself telling the dog, as if she were in the habit of conversing with animals. ''I'm here to straighten things out. He's not going anywhere.''

As soon as the words were out, J.D. appeared in the doorway with a stack of wood cradled on one arm and the handle of a duffel bag gripped in his other hand.

Even frowning the way he was now, he looked so appealing that Kirby's heart stuttered and then resumed a ragged beat. Oh, Lord, but she'd missed him.

"What are you doing here?" he asked bluntly.

She didn't answer immediately. She'd seen him only a couple of times all week and then from a distance. Now his presence wiped her brain clean of everything she'd planned to say.

"Please don't go," she pleaded instead as he walked past her and tossed his belongings into the back of the truck.

"I have to."

"Why? Don't you think we deserve a chance to work things out?"

He shook his head slowly. "It's better this way, for both of us." There was pain in his eyes, and she wondered if he could see its reflection on her own face.

"No," she contradicted, suddenly filled with an icy calm. "That's where you're wrong. This is *not* better for me."

"I have to do this." His jaw was bunched and a muscle worked in his cheek. He glanced around and she knew he was getting ready to bolt. "Maybe it's better for me."

"Where are you going?"

He shrugged. "I haven't thought that far ahead."

Kirby's heart surged into her throat. She couldn't let him leave, not like this. "Take me with you." The words surprised her nearly as much as they obviously did him.

They were barely out of her mouth before he started shaking his head. "No, it wouldn't work. I don't even have a job lined up."

"I'm a nurse," she said. "I can find work anywhere."

He thrust out his jaw, reminding her of one of her nephews. "I am what I am. That may never change.

I have no idea where I'll end up or what I'll be doing, but it probably won't be anyplace you'd want to be.''

"I want to be wherever you are," she insisted.

For a moment, he looked at her hungrily. Her heart surged. Then he shook his head. "You have family here. You belong with them.''

"I belong with you. I love you.''

Emotion flickered across his face. "Love can die. I couldn't bear to watch that happen, waiting for you to get fed up and leave.'' He hung his head. "I couldn't bear it, and I can't stand the idea of waiting around for it to happen.''

"I believe in you,'' she insisted.

"You only believe in something you're trying to turn me into.'' He thumped his chest with his fist. "What I am isn't enough for you.'' His derisive tone should have angered her; instead it made her want to cry. Deciding to do neither, she turned around and went back to the Bronco.

J.D. watched her get in and drive away, feeling as though his heart had been ripped out and was being dragged down the road behind her. He'd been right to refuse to take her with him, even though he'd been tempted more than he'd ever been before in his life to scoop her into his arms and do just that.

His shoulders drooped as he thought of never seeing her again, never holding her or kissing her, never hearing her say she loved him. For a moment his eyes filled, blinding him. Just this one time he'd heard her, and the memory of it would have to last him for the rest of his life.

Snake was watching him steadily from his one yellow eye. J.D. hadn't figured out yet what to do about the dog. Maybe he'd run down to the bunkhouse and ask Cookie if he'd feed him. The man had two big dogs of his own; maybe he'd agree.

Meanwhile, J.D. had a few things left to pack. Impatiently, he swiped at his eyes. Jaw clenched, he headed up the steps.

When he came back out, Snake was gone, too. Just as well, he thought; it would save him telling the animal goodbye. He was better off alone. The only one he'd ever been able to count on, the only one he ever needed, was himself.

Kirby burst in the back door of the house, grateful to see her brother and his wife sitting at the kitchen table. At her sudden entrance, they both looked up expectantly.

"Any luck?" Donovan asked.

"I'm going with him," she announced.

"Good for you," Bobbie exclaimed.

"Where are you headed?" Donovan asked, forehead furrowed with concern.

"I don't know and I don't have time to explain. I have to pack a few things."

"You're leaving now?" Bobbie exclaimed.

"Did J.D. *ask* you to go with him?" Donovan demanded.

"Not exactly."

"Did he *agree* to take you with him?" her brother persisted.

She bit her lip. "Not exactly."

He slid back his chair. "Maybe I'd better go down there with you and talk to him." He didn't look as if he could be easily dissuaded, and she didn't have a lot of time.

"First I need to pack," she said, heading for the

hallway. She wasn't surprised when Bobbie followed her to the bedroom.

"Don't try to talk me out of this," Kirby warned as she emptied underwear into her small suitcase.

"Honey, I wouldn't dream of it."

Kirby glanced up from the nightgown she was folding. "Why not?" she asked suspiciously.

Bobbie shrugged. "Because you're following your heart. I don't imagine I could talk you out of it if I tried. And I wouldn't want to."

For a moment, Kirby struggled with emotions that threatened to spill over. "You're the sister I never had," she said finally, reaching out her arms as tears spilled over and ran down her cheeks. The two women hugged briefly and then Kirby went back to her packing, wiping at her cheeks as she did. Opening her top drawer, she got her bank book. Donovan had refused to take any rent from her, so she'd been saving money from each paycheck. From the sound of things, she and J.D. were going to need it.

"I'll tell Rose goodbye for you," Bobbie offered.

Kirby hesitated guiltily. "Do you think she'll be upset? She did say she was going to marry him, you know."

Bobbie grinned. "Yesterday she confided in me that she had a little talk with him. About you."

Kirby stared. "You're kidding. Did she elaborate?" Had it been something Rose said that had him running away like this?

"No, only that since she won't be grown-up for years and years and he's lonely now, she advised him to marry you."

"Apparently he didn't listen," Kirby replied dryly,

"Well, when you tell her goodbye for me, thank her for trying."

"Okay." Bobbie stepped aside and followed Kirby down the staircase. Donovan was waiting at the bottom.

"Don't worry about the Bronco," he said. "If you can't take it now, we'll just keep it here for you until you need it."

"Thanks. And call my boss at the nursing agency, would you? Tell her—"

"I'll explain the situation," he interrupted. "Hadn't we better get going?"

"You really don't have to go with me."

"I know, but I have my reasons."

She didn't have the time to argue. Instead, she gave Bobbie a goodbye hug and hurried outside. Snake was there waiting for her. When he saw her, he wagged his tail tentatively.

"Yes," she told him. "I'm going." When she held up the suitcase as if to show it to him, he barked and twirled in a circle. Perhaps he wanted to go with them as well.

Donovan took the suitcase from her and suggested they walk. "J.D. has to pass us to leave the ranch," he said. "We aren't going to miss him, and I don't think he'd run us down while we're on foot." He reached out to trace a line down Kirby's cheek with his finger. "Honey, I hate losing you so soon after I finally got you back. Are you sure about this?"

"As I've ever been about anything," she replied, gripping his hand in hers. "And you won't lose me again. No matter what happens, I promise I'll stay in touch."

His smile was a balm to her heart. "Okay. Let's go."

When they got to J.D.'s house, he was just closing the tailgate of his pickup. He glanced up at them warily, and then his eyes widened when he saw the suitcase.

"What's going on?"

Kirby walked over to where he was standing and dropped the suitcase at his feet. "I'm coming with you," she announced. "So you might as well find a place for this."

"That's ridiculous." He started to walked around her, and Snake, who'd positioned himself between J.D. and the driver's door of his pickup, growled low in his throat, lips curled back to reveal huge yellow teeth.

Astonished, J.D. stumbled to a halt and gaped at the dog.

"You can't argue with everyone," Kirby said, walking past Snake, who quieted immediately, and opening the door of the truck. "You might as well give in."

J.D. cast an angry glance at Donovan, who hadn't said a word. "You going to try to talk her out of this, Buchanan? She's your sister."

"She's your girlfriend." Donovan reached for his wallet. "I wanted to settle up with you on your pay."

Surprised, J.D. stilled his hand. "You paid me already."

"You're leaving Popcorn behind, so I owe you a refund." He pulled out some bills and began counting them off.

"Would you just keep her for me instead?" J.D.

asked. "I'll let you know what to do with her when I get settled somewhere."

"Sure, if that's what you want." Donovan held out the money. "Why don't you take this anyway, just in case? Call it a loan, if you like."

"I've got enough," J.D. said hoarsely, "but thanks."

Donovan searched his face, then smiled and tucked the bills back into his wallet. "Whatever you say." He held out his hand. Kirby was relieved when J.D. shook it.

Then Donovan turned to her and opened up his arms. "You need anything, either of you, don't hesitate to call," he said when he'd released her.

"I haven't agreed to take her," J.D. stated.

"I'll leave the two of you to work that out," Donovan replied. With a last smile, he began walking back down the road.

As soon as he was out of sight, J.D. parked his fists on his hips and glowered at Kirby. "I don't know where I'm headed," he began.

"I don't care."

His eyes narrowed. "I don't know what will happen." His voice rose. "I can't guarantee that I'll ever amount to anything."

"You already are!" she shouted, frustration creeping into her voice. "You're everything I need. I love you."

For a moment, he merely stood there with his head thrown back and his eyes squeezed shut. "I can't bear thinking you'll leave me someday," he admitted. "Or that you'll stop loving me."

"I won't. I promise." A little of the chill around her heart was starting to thaw.

He sighed as he looked down at her. "What am I going to do with you?"

"Just love me back," she replied.

His smile was crooked as he shook his head slowly. "Ah, honey, I do," he admitted softly. "But it's almost Christmas, and you'd be leaving your family. You deserve to spend the holidays with them."

At his heartfelt words, Kirby's eyes filled with tears of mingled joy and relief. "I belong with you," she told him, "and you aren't going without me."

J.D. didn't move, didn't speak. He appeared to be having some kind of internal battle with himself. "You'd give all this up for me?" He made a sweeping gesture with his hand.

Shaking with need, the tears rolling freely down her face, Kirby said in a strangled voice, "I believe in you. And in our love. Can't you believe in us, too?"

For a moment he remained where he was. Then, to her utter amazement, he fell to his knees in the muddy snow at her feet. He tipped back his head and she saw that his eyes were glazed with moisture. "I do believe in us," he whispered in a harsh voice. "I love you."

Overjoyed, Kirby threw her arms around his neck and buried her face in his hair. "There's something else," he said in a muffled voice.

Instantly wary, she released him and stepped back to look into his face. "What is it?" What else could there be?

"Would you consider marrying me as soon as we can arrange it?" he asked. "I have no idea what the future holds, so you don't have to if you don't—"

With a shriek, she grabbed him again, almost toppling him over. "Yes," she exclaimed, covering his face with kisses. "Oh, yes, of course I will."

Deeply moved by her faith in him, J.D. suddenly realized there was no longer any real reason for either of them to leave. He'd thought he couldn't stay, knowing she was up at the house, wondering when he'd run into her, but now everything was changed. If she could offer to give up her family for him, couldn't he put aside his pride and ask Donovan for his job back? Ask Jonathan if he was still willing to deal with him at the gallery?

"Would you like to stay here?" he asked, slowly getting to his feet.

Her eyes darkened. "I told you I'd go with you."

Gently, he touched her cheek with his knuckles. "City girl, I meant that we could both stay here, at least until I apologize to Jonathan. Wouldn't you like to spend Christmas with your family?"

"You'd work with him again?" she asked. "Even after what I did?"

He couldn't hold back his smile. "Honey, you did it for me. You knew I was too stubborn to see a good thing that was right in front of my nose. I gave you little choice."

"That isn't quite true," she replied. "But thank you for saying it. I know Jonathan will be thrilled. He thanked me over and over for putting him in touch with you." She threaded her arms around his neck. "He believes in you, too. A lot of people do."

J.D. wrapped his arm around her waist and pulled her close. "I'm beginning to see that. As long as you do, though, that's all that really matters."

Before he let her go, he leaned down and gave her gentle kiss, trying to put all the feelings rushing through him into it. Then he let her go and took her hand.

"Let's go tell your family," he suggested, "and then I'll hit your other brother up for my old job. I don't think he's filled it yet."

As they walked down the road, J.D. glanced back and began to chuckle. Following them was Snake, tongue lolling and tail wagging. He looked the happiest that J.D. had ever seen him.

Epilogue

One year later

"Your daddy will be back soon," Kirby crooned
to her infant son as he waved one tiny fist.

Solemnly he stared back at her with dark eyes that
reminded her of his father's. Adam Chee Reese blew
a bubble and clutched the finger she held out to him.
Humming softly, Kirby got to her feet and raised him
to her shoulder as she stepped around a stack of cardboard cartons and crossed to the living-room window.

She could hardly believe it had been over a year
since she and J.D. had almost left here the first time,
and now they were nearly ready to leave for real. The
house and workshop they'd built on land Donovan
had given them for a wedding present was finally
complete, and they were moving in tomorrow. J.D.

had taken a load of his tools over to the huge workshop this afternoon.

She was still humming tunelessly to Adam when Snake rose from his cushion in the corner of the small living room and cocked his head, whining softly. The dog still slept beneath the porch at night, but he liked to spend the day in the house now if anyone else was home.

"Do you hear the truck?" Kirby asked him.

When he barked once in response, she hurried toward the back door with Adam in her arms. She never failed to feel a rush of excitement when J.D. came in the door.

In minutes, J.D. had kissed the two of them and hung his heavy jacket and black Stetson on the coat rack.

"Did you get your tools arranged to your satisfaction?" Kirby asked him as he patted Snake's head and reached for Adam.

"I can hardly believe I'll have all that room to work," he replied. "Jonathan's been bugging me to do some bigger pieces and now I can." Gently, he tucked the baby into the crook of his arm, gazing down at his dark head with a bemused smile that never failed to give Kirby a surge of pure happiness. He'd assisted her at the delivery, reminding her at the time that she'd trained him herself at Anna Szabo's months before. It was still difficult for him to share with her his innermost thoughts and feelings, but he was opening up more all the time, and she was learning to read him fairly well.

"Did your mother call?" he asked as he looked up and smiled at her.

"Yes, she did. She and Dad want to come out as

soon as we're settled in the new house. And she asked if we have any new pictures of Adam." Kirby and J.D. had visited the Wilsons in Boise shortly after their wedding the year before. The breach she'd still felt at the time had been partially healed by their ready acceptance of her new husband. They'd come to Colorado twice since then, for a major showing of J.D.'s creations at Jonathan's gallery in Aspen, and later to see their new grandson for the first time.

"I have something for you," J.D. said as he handed Adam back to her. "It's upstairs. Wait here and I'll bring it down."

Puzzled, Kirby sat down on the couch, watching Adam struggle to keep his eyes open. It was nearly time for his feeding and nap. When he was home, J.D. liked to sit in the big rocker he'd made for the nursery and hold Kirby while she nursed.

In moments, J.D. had come back down the stairs carrying a large, flat package wrapped in brown paper. Curious, Kirby lay Adam down on his blanket next to her and began opening the package while J.D. stood over her.

"It's something for the new house," he said with barely suppressed excitement when she glanced up.

Carefully, she opened the wrapping and gazed down at the wall plaque that was revealed. On it was carved the image of a woman seated in a rocking chair, nursing her baby. At the woman's feet sat a man whose long hair was tied back with a leather thong. On his face J.D. had managed to capture all the unspoken emotion she knew to be in her husband's loving and generous heart.

Kirby looked up with fresh tears in her eyes. "It's wonderful," she murmured.

J.D. knelt down beside her and laid his head in her lap. "Thank you for loving me," he whispered hoarsely.

Heart full, Kirby put a hand on his head and gently stroked his hair, as little Adam snored softly beside them.

*   *   *   *   *

ERICA SPINDLER

the bestselling author of
FORTUNE and FORBIDDEN FRUIT

Outrageous and unconventional, Veronique Delacroix is an illegitimate child of one of the oldest and wealthiest families in New Orleans. A gambler by nature, Veronique can never say no to a challenge... especially from Brandon Rhodes, heir to one of the biggest business empires in the country. Thus begins a daring game of romantic roulette, where the stakes may be too high....

"Erica Spindler is a force to be reckoned with in the romance genre." —*Affaire de Coeur*

CHANCES ARE

Available in May 1997 at your favorite retail outlet.

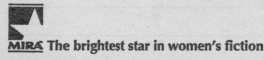

Take 4 bestselling love stories FREE

Plus get a FREE surprise gift!

Special Limited-time Offer

Mail to Silhouette Reader Service™

3010 Walden Avenue
P.O. Box 1867
Buffalo, N.Y. 14240-1867

YES! Please send me 4 free Silhouette Special Edition® novels and my free surprise gift. Then send me 6 brand-new novels every month, which I will receive months before they appear in bookstores. Bill me at the low price of $3.34 each plus 25¢ delivery and applicable sales tax, if any.* That's the complete price and a savings of over 10% off the cover prices—quite a bargain! I understand that accepting the books and gift places me under no obligation ever to buy any books. I can always return a shipment and cancel at any time. Even if I never buy another book from Silhouette, the 4 free books and the surprise gift are mine to keep forever.

235 BPA A3UV

Name _____ (PLEASE PRINT) _____

Address _____ Apt. No. _____

City _____ State _____ Zip _____

This offer is limited to one order per household and not valid to present Silhouette Special Edition® subscribers. *Terms and prices are subject to change without notice. Sales tax applicable in N.Y.

USPED-696   ©1990 Harlequin Enterprises Limited

At last the wait is over...
In March
New York Times bestselling author

NORA ROBERTS

will bring us the latest from the Stanislaskis as
Natasha's now very grown-up stepdaughter,
Freddie, and Rachel's very sexy brother-in-law
Nick discover that love is worth waiting for in

WAITING FOR NICK

Silhouette Special Edition #1088

and in April
visit Natasha and Rachel again—or meet them
for the first time—in

The Stanislaski Sisters

containing TAMING NATASHA
and FALLING FOR RACHEL

Available wherever Silhouette books are sold.

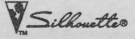

As seen on TV!
Free Gift Offer

With a Free Gift proof-of-purchase from any Silhouette® book,
you can receive a beautiful cubic zirconia pendant.

This gorgeous marquise-shaped stone is a genuine cubic
zirconia—accented by an 18" gold tone necklace.

(Approximate retail value $19.95)

Send for yours today...
compliments of *Silhouette*®

To receive your free gift, a cubic zirconia pendant, send us one original proof-of-purchase, photocopies not accepted, from the back of any Silhouette Romance™, Silhouette Desire®, Silhouette Special Edition®, Silhouette Intimate Moments® or Silhouette Yours Truly™ title available in February, March and April at your favorite retail outlet, together with the Free Gift Certificate, plus a check or money order for $1.65 U.S./$2.15 CAN. (do not send cash) to cover postage and handling, payable to Silhouette Free Gift Offer. We will send you the specified gift. Allow 6 to 8 weeks for delivery. Offer good until April 30, 1997 or while quantities last. Offer valid in the U.S. and Canada only.

Free Gift Certificate

Name: _____

Address: _____

City: _____ State/Province: _____ Zip/Postal Code: _____

Mail this certificate, one proof-of-purchase and a check or money order for postage and handling to: SILHOUETTE FREE GIFT OFFER 1997. In the U.S.: 3010 Walden Avenue, P.O. Box 9077, Buffalo NY 14269-9077. In Canada: P.O. Box 613, Fort Erie, Ontario L2Z 5X3.

FREE GIFT OFFER   084-KFD
ONE PROOF-OF-PURCHASE
To collect your fabulous FREE GIFT, a cubic zirconia pendant, you must include this original proof-of-purchase for each gift with the properly completed Free Gift Certificate.

084-KFD

In April 1997
Bestselling Author

DALLAS SCHULZE

takes her Family Circle series to new heights with

TESSA'S CHILD

In April 1997 Dallas Schulze brings readers a
brand-new, longer, out-of-series title featuring the
characters from her popular Family Circle miniseries.

When rancher Keefe Walker found Tessa Wyndham he
knew that she needed a man's protection—she was
pregnant, alone and on the run from a heartless past.
Keefe was also hiding from a dark past...but in one
overwhelming moment he and Tessa forged a family
bond that could never be broken.

Available in April wherever books are sold.

IN CELEBRATION OF MOTHER'S DAY, JOIN
SILHOUETTE THIS MAY AS WE BRING YOU

a funny thing
HAPPENED ON THE WAY TO THE
Delivery Room

THESE THREE STORIES, CELEBRATING THE
LIGHTER SIDE OF MOTHERHOOD, ARE
WRITTEN BY YOUR FAVORITE AUTHORS:

KASEY MICHAELS
KATHLEEN EAGLE
EMILIE RICHARDS

When three couples make the trip to the delivery
room, they get more than their own bundles of
joy…they get the promise of love!

Available this May,
wherever Silhouette books are sold.

MD